Roxy Buckles
AND THE FLIGHT OF THE SPARROW

Published in Canada by Engen Books, Chapel Arm, NL.

A CIP catalogue record for this book is available from Library and Archives Canada.

ISBN-13: 978-1-77478-110-4

Distributed by:
Engen Books
www.engenbooks.com
submissions@engenbooks.com

First mass market paperback printing: September 2022

Cover Design: Ellen Curtis
Cover Image: Kate Cunningham

Roxy Buckles
AND THE FLIGHT OF THE SPARROW

NICOLE LITTLE

ENGEN
BOOKS

For my grandmother
Susie Little
who encouraged my love of books.

And, as always, for Bridget and Suzie.

CHAPTER ONE

Suki's eyes widened and shock spread across her face in discernable waves as she took in the gruesome sight before her; it ended at her mouth, which had taken on the shape of a perfect O.

"I know. I know." Roxy grimaced. "Shower-to-go isn't going to fix this, is it?"

"No chance in hell."

They stared at each other; neither blinked.

"It's starting to dry." A pause. "I think."

Roxy swiped a hand across her forehead and Suki watched in horrified fascination as a thick black glob rolled down Roxy's cheek and along her jawline. It quivered obscenely at the peak of her chin for a fraction of a second, and then hit the floor with an audible plop.

"Guess not."

"Get out! Go now!" Suki roared. "We're going to need a hazmat crew if you keeping dripping that... *stuff* all over the place."

Roxy shrugged helplessly, the movement dislodging even more gunk from somewhere beneath her jacket. She began to slink backwards out of the room, cringing at the ropy footprints she was leaving behind.

Suki's nostrils flared.

"Now I'm going to have to clean that up." The words, a low growl, reminded Roxy of exactly why she never wanted to be on Suki Kwan's bad side. "I don't like cleaning."

"I'm sorry Suki. Really!" she implored. "But what about the Witchlet meeting? I can't miss that."

"I'll have Mrs. Lester wait in your office for a few minutes once she arrives. She won't mind. Now go!"

"Go *where* exactly?"

"Down to transport. I'll just let them know you're on the way." She tapped a few keys on her wristlet communicator and with deadpan delivery: "They can hose you down with one of the Zip Ship power washers."

"One of the wha…" The auto-door swished shut on Roxy's startled expression and Suki snorted.

She wheeled her chair out from behind the desk and towards the hall closet, seeking out their meagre cleaning supplies: a threadbare mop and a spray bottle of funky green chemicals. Suki gave a long-suffering sigh. It would have to do.

"Revenge is a dish best served cold Roxy Buckles," Suki muttered, as she scrubbed ineffectually at the mess on the floor. "Cold and *wet*."

***

Roxy paused for effect outside the automatic

doors, then, with as much dignity as she could muster, flounced inside - she was still dripping.

Much to Suki's relief, it was just water this time.

Roxy's short blonde curls were dark with moisture and she was fresh-faced, scrubbed of the dark mascara and bold red lipstick she favored. She was clad in a faded mechanic's suit: she'd left the overalls open at the neck and had rolled the bottoms up to mid-calf; she was barefoot. Suki watched with rapt attention as a droplet of water slid from a ringlet of Roxy's hair and trickled its way down into ...

"Like what you see?"

Roxy smirked and sashayed past Suki.

"Roxy..."

Roxy paused, and waited for the apology she felt sure was coming.

"You smell *so* much better now."

The reply came swiftly, in the shape of one perfectly manicured finger. Suki dissolved into a fit of laughter.

Roxy stopped, just short of the door, her voice indignant but lowered in deference to the client waiting in the next room, "I cannot *believe* you had them *hose* me down like I was some sort of... of... *soiled* vehicle."

Suki stifled her giggles, chagrined, and raised her hands in defeat. "I'm sorry Roxy, it was the quickest way I could think of to clean you up."

Roxy groaned dramatically and gestured to what she was wearing. "Not very professional now is it?"

"I am absolutely certain that Ethel-Beth Lester

doesn't care what you are wearing as long as you do your job." She lowered her voice even further: "Do you think you'll be able to bring him back this time?"

Roxy's face was grim. "My theory? He's been served up for lunch long before now." She sighed. "But I suppose there's always a chance. So, I have to try. He might have hooked up with a Witchlet who's particularly sadistic. She might try to make it last a little longer, use him up for a couple of days to savour the kill. I guess I'll bring back whatever I can find."

She shrugged as she stepped away, plastered a smile on her face, opened the door to the inner office and closed it behind her with a faint click.

Ethel-Beth Lester sat waiting, patient as always, in one of the supple leather chairs placed in front of Roxy's desk. The woman gazed out the window, lost in thought, her mouth set in a thin line. Roxy cleared her throat softly so as not to startle her. She flinched anyways.

"Good day to you Mrs. Lester. I apologize for making you wait. I was slightly… indisposed. But now, I am prepped and ready for my trip to Salemmas. Once I know more about the situation, I will have someone contact you immediately. Most likely my associate Ms. Kwan."

She was but a wisp of a thing, Mrs. Lester, but Roxy knew there was a steely resolve beneath the soft exterior. "Thank you.

Roxy ran a finger along the inside of the coarse collar of her borrowed overalls. The tag at the back was irritating her neck. Who would wear these damned things by choice? The boorish mechanic hadn't been too keen on handing over the extra suit but his interest had definitely been piqued when he realized that Roxy intended to strip out of her saturated clothes right where she was standing. Her polite request that he avert his eyes while she did so had been met with some reluctance.

So, she'd thrown a wrench at him.

Okay, several wrenches.

She figured he was probably still running.

Roxy would get Suki to report the incident to Marcus MacLeod, head of building security and the man in charge of operating systems, before he left for the day. She could not do her job effectively if she was surrounded by a bunch of degenerates. Throwing tools at tools was not a part of her job description.

"Do you think Charles is still alive?" Mrs. Lester's soft voice snapped her back to the present.

"I wouldn't be able to say for sure, not until I see for myself. The length of the courting process varies, as you know, but we may still have a small window of opportunity." She paused, uncertain whether she would be crossing the line if she continued: "Look, I like you Mrs. Lester, so I am going to be straight with you because I don't want to give you false hope. This is the third time Mr. Lester has left with a Witchlet. If I can find him… are you sure you even want him back?"

To her surprise, Ethel-Beth laughed. "I wonder

the same thing myself sometimes Ms. Buckles. I suppose I'm stubborn. I'm not ready to give up on him just yet."

"Then I will do my best."

"I know you will Ms. Buckles. You always do. Thank you once again for all your help."

"My pleasure," Roxy replied.

Roxy followed Mrs. Lester out of the room. She frowned as the doors slid shut behind what was her most frequent client. She hoped would be able to do right by her. *Damn you Charles Lester*.

Roxy's job as an Exterminator, a bounty hunter-cum-mercenary, was not always pleasant. In fact, it very rarely was. Chasing down toxic pests, aliens, and invasive species was only one small part of her repertoire. Sometimes she had to go after the big guns, the worst criminals imaginable, and sometimes, things got a little dirty. People came to her during the worst moments of their lives and she tried to make things a little better when she could. She wanted to bring back good news and lost loved ones to their family members but, sometimes, the best she could do was a handful of scorched remains.

She closed the office door behind her and turned her attention to Suki Kwan, bouncing in her chair with excitement.

"Roxy." Suki gestured towards her desk. A flat rectangular package sat there. "I got a little something for you - a peace offering. The delivery drone dropped it off a short while ago. I gave very specific instructions to the boutique so; I hope you like it."

Roxy opened the embossed white box and eagerly removed a pair of form fitting black pants, a sleek red body suit and a cropped black leather jacket. She could not have chosen better herself.

Those overalls were history.

"You are the absolute best." She leaned over and pressed a loud affectionate kiss on Suki's cheek.

"Are you blushing Suki Kwan?"

"No. Absolutely not. Now enough of this mushy shit. The Zip Ship is fueled up and ready to go, so... go!"

CHAPTER TWO

Salemmas was distant, dark and desolate, a planet found nestled along the Daemon Belt. One of the least hospitable in the solar system, they welcomed visitors not with open arms but with open mouths and bared teeth.

At least it's not Mars, Roxy thought to herself, shuddering. She hated those damn dinosaurs.

The Zip Ship hovered, just above the Salemmas stratosphere, as Roxy doused the landing lights and prepared for descent. She would have to go in blind for this one. It was fortunate for Roxy, and for Ethel-Beth Lester, that Roxy was an acquaintance of the High Queen Witchlet Moll and as such, was permitted to come and go when necessary. There would be no fear of reprisal from the vicious creatures, but still, she was reluctant to announce her arrival. Roxy rarely set foot on the miserable planet and then, only when she had been hired to do an extraction. The hazard pay she planned to tack onto this particular invoice wouldn't hurt either.

This sort of job was usually grab and go; quick

and dirty and usually not very successfully. At least for the women who hired her. Roxy's return trips to Aurora often saw her accompanied by nothing more than a small box of scraps; perhaps a fingernail or a tooth, a button from a shirt. If she was lucky enough to find anything at all.

She maneuvered through the cloud cover and eased the ship down onto the unfamiliar soil. It was black as death, despite the fact that it was mid-day. Tall, barren trees, their pale bark luminescent even in the dim light, towered overhead, their branches bowing outward in a tangled canopy over clusters of small dome shaped structures. These, Roxy knew, were the nurseries. From a distance, she could see the bright red lights of the main habitat - a large low unattractive building that did not inspire a welcome. She knew that deep below the rudimentary structure there were intricate tunnel systems, leading off into cavernous rooms where the Witchlets lived in groups of three. The nurseries, where the younglings were incubated, had to be kept near the outer limits of the planet to ensure the safety of the little ones. If a Witchlet were hungry enough or simply in the mood for fresh meat… well, it was better to remove temptation completely. Witchlets had enough population problems as it was.

Roxy exited the Zip Ship, landed solidly on her feet and remained in a crouch; she edged her way across the uneven terrain, trying to ignore the eerie snuffles and shrieks inside the nursery as she passed. Her fingers hovered at the weapon holstered on her hip. She knew from experience how painful a Witchlet nip could be and hoped she would never have to experience that again.

Her plan was to approach with caution initially, do re-con, and figure out what approach was necessary. Taking a quick glance inside the smudged windows, she saw workers in aprons busily placing bowls and plates along a banquet table; brightly colored fruits and lush green vegetables edged around the buffet. The focus though seemed to be on the middle of the table - the pièce de resistance - which had already been greased up, plump and prepped for roasting.

The pièce de resistance was, of course, Charles Lester.

His face bore an expression of dreamy disconnect; he lay there contentedly, simply awaiting his fate. The deed was nearly done. His purpose nearly fulfilled.

That decided it. Roxy breached the entrance with a stiff kick, a guttural roar escaping her lips. She was a tall woman, but in her high heeled black boots she cut a formidable figure. The Witchlets screamed and scattered as Roxy smashed her way through the entrance. They scurried through the first open doorway they could escape through.

Roxy snorted. Her reputation often preceded her but this was something else entirely.

She walked across the room to give Lester the once over. He seemed relatively unharmed and when she leaned in for a closer look he was still breathing. Witchlet poison was a powerful sedative and while its purpose was to make the victim docile, it very often slowed their heart rate. Sometimes it did a little more than just make the victim compliant.

Distracted, Roxy didn't feel the arm come from behind her until it was wrapped around her neck. The arm wrenched her backwards, knocking over several pieces of crockery. Broken glass and food carpeted the floor beneath their feet.

The fetid exhalations of the Witchlet who'd seen fit to grab her wafted into her face.

Minty fresh, it was not.

"Got youuuu." she intoned, her giggles high pitched and eager.

Roxy rolled her eyes. Yeah, you keep thinking that, fucker, Roxy thought and allowed her attacker to gain confidence - let her think that she was going to win. They waltzed around the room - a macabre dance - squashing mangalo fruit and tomates beneath their feet in the process. The Witchlet tightened her grip on Roxy's neck; her breath was hot and fast in Roxy's ear.

Roxy did not even try to suppress the shudder of revulsion that rocked her as the Witchlet rubbed against her obscenely.

Clearly, she was expecting both dinner *and* dessert tonight.

Okay, bitch, play time is over. Roxy let herself to go limp. As expected, the Witchlet loosened her grip. Before she had a chance to realize that things were about to go *very* wrong for her, Roxy had tossed her to the ground and pinned her there, the Witchlet's arms braced behind her, Roxy's knee in the middle of her shoulders. Subdued.

"Got youuuu." Roxy mimicked.

"Please," came the muffled plea. "I swear I wasn't going to hurt you. It was a joke."

Roxy hissed a breath from between gritted teeth. These bloody things were so exasperating to deal with. Conniving and clever. But not much got past Roxy.

"You seriously cannot expect me to believe that." Roxy retorted; her eyes ablaze. "You attacked me from behind. I think we all know where *that* was headed."

"Okay, fair enough." The Witchlet giggled again, nervously this time. "But in my defense, that was before I realized just who you were."

Roxy tightened her grip, wrenching the Witchlets arms high towards the middle of her back, grinding her knee cap into the Witchlets spine.

"Ow. Stop, please. Okay… Roxy Buckles, right? What if I told you, I have some information that could be very valuable to you?" she stammered, the words running together in her haste to get them out, muffled by the floor and the squashed food her face was pressing into.

"I'd say you were full of shit." Roxy remarked, growing bored with the exchange.

"I swear. It's *good* info. And you're definitely going to want to hear it. All you have to do is let me go and I'll tell you."

Roxy considered the options. She could definitely take on one Witchlet, especially this one, with an arm tied behind her back. But, if she screeched for her coven, then it became a three on one scenario; that would be a problem. Roxy did have to admit, as much as she was sure the Witchlet was having her on, she *was* intrigued.

"If you scream, I'll cut off your -."

"I won't," the Witchlet gulped, knowing exactly what Roxy would cut off.

With a sigh, Roxy released her. The Witchlet scrambled backwards on all fours until she came up against a wall. For all her bravado, she certainly seemed inclined to put some distance between herself and Roxy. The green opalescent scaled skin, long red hair, wickedly sharp nails and pointed teeth

Roxy placed her hand on her weapon; she was curious but she was not stupid.

"What's your name?"

"Verbena."

"And why should I believe anything you have to tell me?"

"I'm a Scout, you see. Queen Moll, she sends me out to different planets looking for ... uh ... companions. There've been a lot of rumours lately. Your name came up several times."

Roxy drew her weapon and spun the dial. It whirred menacingly, it's light flashing through a myriad of colors before it settled on an angry red. It beeped once and a small dot between the Witchlet's two eyes. Roxy took a step closer. Beads of sweat sprung up on Verbena's scaly forehead. She pressed back against the wall.

"Rumours don't pay the bills Verbena."

"It's about a man." She whimpered, really laying it on thick. "He's been on the run a long time. A fugitive. I think you might know him."

Roxy's breath caught in her throat. *Was it possible? Could it really be after all this time?* She wondered. *Dare I hope?*

Abruptly Roxy deactivated and re-holstered her weapon. She crouched down and scrutinized the Witchlet for signs that she was lying. Roxy tried not to appear too eager but the Witchet knew she had her now.

"Talk," Roxy barked, her mood quickly darkening.

Verbena sat forward and eyed Roxy with smug satisfaction.

"Sam Sparrow."

CHAPTER THREE

Charles Lester was still unconscious but his vitals were steady when Roxy returned him home safe and sound. Safe at least until his wife got her hands on him. A sleek Servo-Bot whisked him off down a long hallway while another bot went in search of Mrs. Lester in the stately hover-mansion. Roxy followed along, curiosity getting the better of her once again, and caught a glimpse of a stylish but simple bedroom on the main level.

The Servo-Bot had tucked Mr. Lester into a single bed. Roxy pretended not to notice the bars on the windows or the elaborate locks that had been installed on the outside of the door, though she was impressed by Mrs. Lester's ingenuity and refusal to give in. She quickly retreated, not wanting to get caught snooping by one of her nicest and most lucrative clients.

Mrs. Lester bustled into the foyer a few moments later and offered profuse thanks to Roxy. A small blip from the device around Roxy's wrist indicated that she had been paid in full for her services, plus, she noticed, a generous tip. She bid adieu to the Lester's and silently hoped, for Ethel-Beth's sake, that she would never have to see them again.

The short jaunt across New Cosmos saw Roxy arrive back to the office building quicker than she would have liked. She'd had a lot of time to think between Salemmas and Aurora but she'd also had a lot to process. She sat aboard the Zip as it powered down, wondering how long she'd be able to hide out here before she was discovered.

She'd had a lot of difficult conversations in her lifetime. She'd delivered terrible news to good people; she'd made bad people pay for terrible crimes. But the news she was about to share – it was not a discussion she was looking forward to.

She took a deep breath and unsnapped her seatbelt, slid out of her seat and pushed aside the door before dropping to the ground.

Times like this, she wished there was still something left to pray to.

In lieu of that, there was always liquid courage.

***

The Oasis was blocked. Nothing unusual for this time of night. She tossed back a shot of *Soju* and rapped on the bar for another. Roxy was doing what Roxy did best – avoiding.

Patrons from all walks of life lined the bar, jostling each other amiably while they waited to be served, swaying to the music, shouting to be heard. Roxy didn't have to wait though. She was a good customer, though she usually spent her time there out back, in one of the private suites.

The reverberation of the music beat in tune to Roxy's heart. She closed her eyes, remembering - none to fondly - of a time two years prior when silence had fallen on The Oasis. For a spot where the party never stopped, it was almost a death sentence for the popular establishment.

It wasn't obvious at first, the infestation. The constant flow of intoxicating beverages led to carefree, inebriated revellers; no one took notice of the small winged creatures landing on their arm or their neck, nor the tiny, seemingly insignificant bites of the Succungei. Native to the darkest regions beyond the Daemon Belt, the minuscule vampire-like spider, fond of human blood, secreted poison in its saliva as it licked a wound clean. It caused a painful allergic reaction. The fever hit first, then a swelling of the face and watery blisters; bleeding from the eyes and ears was the final sign. These major symptoms lasted only forty-eight hours but those who suffered from the effects of the poison were often left to deal with vision and hearing issues for years to come.

The Oasis was inundated – both with Succungei and angry victims.

The owners, Lars and Bell, were desperate to save their business, and to ensure the safety and comfort of their loyal patrons. All they needed was someone willing to take on the enormous task of exterminating the building.

Enter Roxy Buckles. She enjoyed a challenge and a challenge this would be, she was absolutely certain.

Slathered in a thick layer of her own patented No-Bite body spray, Roxy was able to enter The Oasis and easily eradicate the space of its smallest invaders... but the Queen, well, that was a whole different story. The vast bulbous arachnid, carpeted with wiry gray hairs and eight protuberant eyes, had not gone down without a fuss. Roxy shuddered at the recollection. Sure, there had been a little damage from the flame thrower but Lars and Bell had been so thankful to take back possession of their business, they were willing to over look a few scorch marks.

A pleasant scent of light citrus teased her nose, teased her out of her reverie. Cologne. She opened her eyes. The guy eased himself onto the barstool next to Roxy at the same time the bartender slid another drink in front of her. It was gone within seconds. She hoped he would be too. She wasn't feeling very social.

"Haven't seen you here before." His voice was gravelly, like he spent a lot of time smoking, or screaming orders. Maybe a bit of both.

"That's because I like to drink alone."

"Fair enough," he held out his hand. "Alexzander S. Zillinger."

Roxy ignored it. "That's a bit of a mouthful."

He winked. "My friends call me Zillo."

"Is your next line going to be something about me needing to know your name 'cause I'll be screaming it later?" Roxy deadpanned.

He threw back his head, his raucous laughter discernible even above the pulse of the music. "I like you. Let me buy you a drink. No strings attached; I promise."

Roxy turned to face him. He had dark eyes and dark hair and the grin on his face suggested knowledge of dark and dirty deeds.

Just the way she liked 'em.

"Okay, I'll have a drink with you. But I buy my own." Roxy waved to the bartender. "I'll take the bottle Suzie, just put it on my tab." She crooked a finger at Zillo. "Let's grab a booth in the back."

***

The bottle in the middle of the table held only an inch of clear liquid. Roxy had consumed most of it. The tension had finally seeped from her shoulders and she was starting to forget her troubles. She let go, began to enjoy herself, the company and the conversation. It had been a long time since she had talked this much.

She was having fun.

She might have been a little bit drunk.

"Wait, you're telling me the guy was keeping a *LanQuid*... in his *bathtub*?" Zillo stared at Roxy, a bemused quirk to his brow. "You know I've always wanted to visit Earth but now I'm not so sure."

"Ah they're not all bad. Maybe just a little naïve." Roxy smiled as she thought of Ed Farris and wondered how the poor guy was doing. And if he'd ever gotten the LanQuid ichor out of his carpet. "We all are, at times."

He watched her, shrewd, assessing. "This ex of

yours. He's on the up and up then?"

Roxy nodded slowly, the liquor had loosened her tongue and she'd confessed the whole sordid mess. "Sure is," a heavy sigh escaped her lips. "I fucked up."

"Don't blame yourself. You did the best you could with the information you had at the time. I bet he doesn't blame you for it either."

She fiddled with her glass, "maybe."

"Think you'll get back together with him after all this is over?"

"I'm afraid that ship has sailed Zillo."

"That's a real shame, doll. Sounds like you really cared for each other."

"Maybe," a shrug of her shoulder. "It is what it is."

They sat in companionable silence for while, the beat of the music throbbing in their ears, the *Sujo* coursing through Roxy's veins.

"Well, Roxy, it's getting late." Zillo cocked his head to one side, pursed his lips. "What do you say we head back to your place now?"

"I think that's the best idea I've heard all day," Roxy replied.

They stood. Zillo threw an arm around Roxy's shoulders and she leaned into his side with a sigh, her head on his shoulder. They left the bar together and headed off into the falling dusk.

***

"You going to be okay to get upstairs by yourself?

I can walk you up if you're feeling too wobbly."

"I'll be fine Zillo, thanks." She hiccupped, then giggled. "Oops. Sorry. I really appreciate the ride home and the chat. It was good to get it off my chest. I've never met an Engineer that didn't drink before."

"One's my limit. Get some sleep doll. Keep in touch, and like I said, call me if you ever need anything. Or even if you don't need anything at all." Zillo winked and pulled away. "Stay safe," he shouted out the window.

Roxy waved. *Who knew?* she thought to herself, *guess you really could find friends in low places.*

***

She flopped back on her bed, fully clothed; let her eyes drift shut. It was certainly not the way Roxy had expected the night to end. *Or the morning to begin*, she thought ruefully to herself as the first pale streaks of dawn penetrated the room, caressing her face with weak sunlight. She turned on her side and curled into a ball. A few hours of sleep were all she needed.

The jarring bleep from her wristlet pulled her back from the edge of slumber. She sat up abruptly, noting the name of the caller on the display. She groaned.

"What's up?"

The voice on the other end of the call was brisk, but Roxy listened attentively, eventually nodding and rising to her feet.

"I'm on my way."

CHAPTER FOUR

Sam Sparrow was dead.

Deceased, departed, lifeless, gone.

Or at least he *would* be... once Roxy caught up with him. He'd finally been spotted. A credible tip from a reliable source this time. It checked out and there would be no mistakes this time.

Yeah, you've already made enough of those, she thought to herself.

This might be her last chance to set things right and she planned to grab that opportunity by the balls. And twist.

Roxy had always thought Sparrow had had help with his escape. She'd never been able to pinpoint just who had been his accomplice but that person was second in line on her most wanted list.

She perched on the corner of her desk, tossed back a third caf-tab and prayed it would keep her upright and moving for the rest of the day. She drummed the fingers of her right-hand rhythmically atop the gleaming surface and stared through the glass windows of her high-rise office. The hazy azure sky proved an inadequate distraction as she ruminated over the logistics of her plan. Her brain was shifting into full prep mode as she neared go time.

There was just that one last little thing that she needed to do.

She couldn't put it off any longer.

"Suki," she shouted through the closed door, the slight waver in her voice only a small indication of the trepidation she felt. This would be a difficult discussion. She waited a few minutes, then louder, "SUKI."

In short order the door banged open and a harried Suki Kwan appeared at the threshold, hands clenched on the wheels of her chair as she pushed herself forward. "You know; you *could* call me on the intercom occasionally. I distinctly remember showing you how to use it, so you have no excuse."

Roxy chuckled, "but how else would I get to see that gorgeous face of yours?"

The quirk of an eyebrow but no response.

Roxy tried again. "I thought you deserved a break?"

The corners of Suki's mouth fought to curl into a smile. A break. Sure. "You're trying to butter me up. What do you want me to do now?"

Roxy paused, her demeanor growing serious. "I need you to clear my schedule for the rest of this week. Maybe even the week after as well."

Suki examined her boss through narrowed eyes, "you're joking."

"Sorry," Roxy said visibly deflated, hoping the

sincerity of her apology came through. "I am not."

Suki was not convinced. She launched into a tirade about responsibilities, their reputation as a company and the potential loss of valuable clients. Roxy winced and collapsed into a chair. She placed her forehead against her cool maple desk and allowed Suki's rage to wash over her. She was right of course but alas... Roxy had to raise her voice several decibels to be heard above the indignation: "I've got a lead on Sparrow."

Silence. Suki Kwan being speechless, that didn't happen very often. Sparrow was a topic they avoided at all costs and here was Roxy just dumping him into the middle of the conversation like a rotting corpse.

Suki's expression ran a gamut of emotions before she quickly composed herself - the defeated slump of her shoulders though; it made Roxy's heart ache. She waited it out, knew Suki would be mad if she intervened with platitudes or pity. When she sensed that Suki was ready, she began to speak again, sharing the information she'd gotten from the Witchlet and the plan she had formulated. It was a damned good plan too.

"Are you sure Roxy?"

"I am."

"It's been such a long time, is it even worth it now?"

"Yes, Suki, it is."

Suki nodded her acceptance. Once Roxy set her mind to something, well, there was no going back.

Roxy stood, with a determined stride she rounded the desk to crouch and take Suki's hand in hers. She brushed her thumb gently across the pale scars that crisscrossed Suki's knuckles: "It will *always* be worth it my friend. You deserve justice. And I sure as hell plan on making sure you get it."

***

Home.

Alone.

With nothing but her thoughts for company.

Nibbling absently on a PWR Protein Delite™, she briefly considered giving in and finally buying herself a robo-pet. Something other than silence to greet her when she walked in the door.

Yes, there were a million other places she would rather be right now than this godforsaken condominium but she had sworn to Suki that she would not leave Aurora until the morning. Transport wouldn't prepare a Zip Ship for her until then anyways. Suki made sure of that.

She frowned at the tasteless snack in her hand, as if only just realizing it was a mediocre excuse for dinner. With a sigh, she tossed it, half eaten, in the trash.

Roxy selected the pre-programmed shutdown mode on her Condo-Comm Interface (or CoCo for short) and the windows overlooking downtown New Cosmos turned opaque and dark. The perfect accompaniment to her mood. A hush fell over the apartment as the state-of-the-art system blocked out the constant rush, rush, rush of the busy metropolis below. All Roxy wanted to hear was the sound of wine being sloshed into a glass. A lot of wine. Into a very large glass. But first, a more adequate shower than the one she had so abruptly received earlier.

She wandered into her bedroom, peeled off the clothes she'd worn that day and with them, her composure.

She stepped into the stall; the one place where she allowed herself to let go, the scalding water washing away the stench of the city, and the scorch of her tears. She scrubbed until her skin was pink.

Afterwards, wrapped in a thigh skimming over-sized sweater and little else, Roxy folded herself onto the sofa, careful not to spill the generous glass of wine she had poured for herself. Using her wristlet, she ordered what would prove to be too much sushi for one person and finally admitted to herself that there was only one thing she would be doing for the rest of the night… and it would not be sleeping.

CHAPTER FIVE

"CoCo, open file A241-M93, cast for display."

"Happy to help, Roxy," came the smooth computerized response. Instantly, the wall in front of Roxy was transformed into a screen and became awash with high resolution photographs. Smiling faces beamed out at her: a blast from the past. She selected one in particular, sweeping aside the others with a flick of her wrist. She grasped the image in mid-air and zoomed in on the happy group.

The good old days. Before everything went to shit.

Roxy waved her hand and the pile of photographs fanned out in front of her again.

"Slideshow."

"Would you like music to accompany your presentation?" CoCo prompted.

"Fuck no."

"As you wish."

The lights dimmed automatically, and in succession, Roxy's early life played out before her eyes. Those blissful years at The Academy, when they were young and unaware just how bad things would get; before they'd experienced horror, loss and sadly, for Roxy, unimaginable betrayal.

She took a hasty sip of wine as a picture of an 18-year-old Suki Kwan came into sharp focus. Roxy's heart swelled. Long, straight, dark hair framed a cherubic face as the vibrant girl posed cheekily against a backdrop of sand and sun. No scars yet marred her perfect complexion. She was happy and healthy. While Suki continued to recover from her injuries, a wheelchair provided freedom and a sense of independence, and as she grew more confident, sometimes just a single cane. Roxy's closest friend. She owed her so much.

Roxy punished herself like this often. Penance. There were some things she just couldn't forgive herself for. Tonight, though, this was different, she was using this to fuel herself for the fight ahead; to get fired up before she would head out in the morning to finally exterminate the one crim that got away.

No one ever escaped from Roxy Buckles. They didn't call her the best in the business for nothing.

And then, there he was, as if her very thoughts had conjured him up out of thin air: winking at her from the slideshow; nearly life-sized, the photo sent shivers coursing down Roxy's spine and the alcohol in her stomach turned sour, the bile rising in her throat.

Sam Sparrow.

"Pause."

She unfurled from her seat, her long legs quickly

bringing her eye to eye with the piece of human garbage who'd nearly stolen everything from her. His
image was already burned into her mind but she still
examined him in great detail, his square jawline, his
aquiline nose and the full lips that stretched across
those perfect white teeth. He was posing with cocky
confidence next to a Zip Ship, the day of their first
practice jaunt; young and brash, and full of promise.

But promises get broken.

A bell jangled loudly. Roxy jumped, her arm jerk-
ing; the wine in her half full glass sloshed over the
rim and spilled. She cursed fluently as red blossomed
across the wall next to her, splattering close to the
ceiling and running in bloody torrents to the floor.

Roxy activated call mode on her wristlet, mentally chastising herself for not having turned off the
damn notification sounds when she had arrived at
home like a sensible person would have done. "Aeyo,
Roxy Buckles speaking."

Eyebrows disappearing somewhere in the vicin-
ity of her hairline, Roxy sat abruptly on the sofa as
the voice on the other end of the wristlet identified
themselves – not that they needed to. Roxy would
have known that voice anywhere. No, it wasn't every
day that she received a personal call from the Commander of the Planetary Regulation Committee.

"Commander Carmine." Roxy tried to keep her
voice even.

"Ms. Buckles. We may have a job for you, if you
are interested."

If she was interested? Roxy thought, astonished

that it was even a question that required any sort of consideration.

"Of course, anything at all I can do to help the Committee sir," Roxy replied, trying to keep her voice level.

"Glad to hear. Please be at The PRC Plaza at nine tomorrow morning. My assistant Flavia will meet you in the lobby."

"I will definitely…" Roxy trailed off at the sound of a loud click. The Commander had already ended the call. "… be there." She ended breathlessly.

Bubbles of anticipation tickled their way through Roxy's stomach, effervescing through her mouth in an exultant shout: "YES."

It had happened. Finally. All her hard work was paying off. Roxy flailed about the room to a song heard only in her head; her arms in the air, her hips gyrating un-rhythmically in what for her was a close approximation of a dance.

Bzzzz.

The takeout food had arrived, interrupting her jubilant celebration. She giggled and straightened her clothes and hair. As she went to answer the buzzer her eyes flicked to the projection still up on the wall and her elation drained away. She slammed back to reality with a jolt and realized with a sinking dread that this meeting with Commander Carmine might mean putting any other plans on hold. *Damn.*

She opened the door and graciously accepted the package of food from the delivery drone. It beeped its thanks and zipped away. Roxy tore into the packaging and, standing at the kitchen counter began devouring her dragon rolls, salmon maki and crab nigari with relish. She washed it down with long pulls of wine from the bottle, swiping her mouth with the back of her hand. All the while she stared daggers at the picture of Sam Sparrow still larger than life on her condo wall, as a crimson stain darkened on the wall behind him.

She nodded decisively.

Soon.

CHAPTER SIX

The next morning, on the mosaic patterned portico that led into The PRC Plaza, Roxy found herself gazing upward in wonder at the unapologetic opulence of the building. The aptly-named *megatall* skyscraper soared beyond the clouds, disappearing into the miasma of morning, its dark tinted windows mirroring distorted ghostly images of passing ships, cargo-carriers and biomorphic robotic birds.

"Excuse me." A tall muscular dual-headed man that Roxy recognized as a local meteorologist grinned at her from both faces as he walked past her on the sidewalk. "Nice day we're having." One head winked and Roxy returned the smile.

It was then she realized that she'd been standing there, slack-jawed in front of the building, for an embarrassing length of time. She clamped her mouth shut and pretended to fiddle with her wristlet until the heat in her cheeks subsided.

She could not - would not - blow this. Ever since she had graduated from the Academy and been given the official designation of Exterminator, she had dreamed of being called upon to serve the Planetary Regulation Committee. And now here she was.

Better late than never, Roxy thought to herself. Stiffening her shoulders, and her resolve, she approached the entryway where the automatic doors whooshed open to permit her access. The chill of the controlled climate inside was a welcome embrace.

The scene that greeted Roxy was absolute chaos. People scurried in all directions and though no one quite seemed to pay attention to where they were going, they avoided each other, and potential collisions, with an ease born of practice.

The place had seen a lot of upgrades since Roxy had last been there a decade ago. That included a large floating electronic notice board that she had to crane her neck to see. Advertisements and announcements flashed across the display.

A tremor passed through Roxy as a large picture of a Witchlet projected onto the screen. She had seen enough of those damned things to last a lifetime. The picture was accompanied by scrolling text encouraging any civilians who had been affected by the recent increase in kidnappings to please contact Sergio in the Complaints Department.

A petite young woman, her short hair the color of ripe blueberries advanced on Roxy, waving impatiently, "I am Flavia, Commander Carmine's executive assistant. Follow me." She turned, not waiting for a response from Roxy, and dashed off in the direction of a bank of elevators nestled in an alcove beneath a busy mezzanine. Roxy followed behind hurriedly, trying to keep Flavia in her sights while she dodged a person swinging a briefcase and shouting loudly into their wrist.

"Level 220," Flavia ordered, barely allowing time for Roxy to slip inside the swiftly closing doors. Roxy shot a surreptitious glance in the assistant's direction; Flavia was staring straight ahead at the floor designators.

The elevator rocketed upwards, numbers blurring on the monitor as the speed increased. Roxy suppressed the urge to fill the awkward silence with small talk and instead, stood quietly, willing her nervous body not to sweat through the armpits of her recently purchased silk charmeuse blouse.

The elevator pinged, announced their arrival, and the doors slid opened. Roxy gaped. The office of Commander Seth Carmine encompassed the entire 220th floor.

"I will leave you here. Please wait in the atrium until you are called." Flavia gestured for Roxy to exit the elevator.

"Thank you."

Flavia gave a curt nod and then she was gone.

Wow. Suki deserves a big raise, Roxy thought.

"Ms. Buckles."

The mellifluous voice came to her from her left and she shifted to acknowledge the tall, well-dressed man who stepped out of the shadows, his hand extended. His thick head of salt and pepper hair was perfectly coiffed. Beneath the curve of his enigmatic smile was a neatly trimmed goatee.

He clasped Roxy's hand in his. His handshake was dry and firm.

"Commander Carmine, it is a pleasure to meet you."

"Ms. Buckles, the pleasure is all mine. Please, join me in the lounge. I've had Flavia come in early and prepare us a breakfast tray. She makes a wonderful cup of coffee."

"I would be delighted and please, call me Roxy."

He grinned. "Excellent. We will be Roxy and Seth then."

Roxy could have fit her entire condo just inside Commander Carmine's lounge. The lavish furnishings were monochrome black and grey; one entire wall was made of glass and looked out onto a tiffany blue sky. The opposite wall was bare, save for a large abstract painting of serpentine swirls.

Feeling strangely out of her element Roxy waited until the Commander indicated she should take a seat before she settled herself on the edge of a stiff leather sofa. A Servo-Bot materialized at Roxy's elbow, poured her a cup of coffee and then dashed away as quickly as it had come. Commander Carmine served himself from a crystal decanter of light amber liquid. Roxy took a small polite sip from her cup; it was good coffee.

"You'll forgive me Roxy if I skip the pleasantries and get straight to business?" He did not wait for a reply. "The PRC have had eyes on a sect of rebels for a while now. Years even. Recently, there have been some rumors of an uprising. They call themselves

The Bastent and we have reason to believe that the recent increase in intergalactic crimes have a direct correlation with their... activism."

Roxy leaned forward; her curiosity piqued. An idea was beginning to take shape in the back of her mind. *Sparrow? Lynx? Was it possible?*

Carmine continued: "Your recent LanQuid problem, for example. Who do you think sent that particular pest Earthside? And I believe there was a rather unpleasant Succungei infestation not that long ago as well? Dare I mention that our Complaints Department is working overtime dealing with all the hysterical women bemoaning the loss of their poor stupid husbands. Damned oversexed aliens." He slammed his glass onto a side table.

"This group has zero interest in negotiating for peace." He grimaced. "We have tried of course, but they are spoiling for war."

"What can I do to..."

"You must infiltrate the contingent." He pushed on, as though he hadn't even heard her speak. "And apprehend their miscreant leader. According to our sources The Bastent have been very, very busy." His upper lip curled in disgust. "Recruiting criminals and other outcasts that they have convinced to commit to their cause. They are running amok all over this solar system and far, far beyond."

Roxy, her coffee long forgotten, placed her cup back on the table. It clinked against the marble top and Commander Carmine jolted. He was so caught up in his impassioned speech, he seemed to have forgotten that there was someone else in the room. He stood and shed his jacket, rolling the sleeves to the elbow. He approached the bank of windows and gazed thoughtfully into the distance. Clouds billowed past, obscuring the view. The silence stretched.

Roxy finally spoke, unable to stand the suspense any longer. "This leader, Commander... Seth... what is..."

"River Lynx." He interrupted, spitting out the name as though it left a bad taste in his mouth. "From Mauw. They have been a thorn in my side for far too long. It's personal now."

Roxy struggled to keep her face blank.

Carmine scrutinized her from across the room. "I am sure you can understand that yourself Roxy. From what I have heard, you know a little something about personal grudges." He stopped just short of a satisfied smirk.

Seth Carmine was a shrewd bastard. But he wouldn't throw Roxy off her game. She knew that her need for vengeance against Sparrow was common knowledge and she could accept that. It also wasn't beyond reason that The PRC would be keeping tabs on her, putting her directly on Carmine's radar.

"I can leave today," she said decisively.

"Excellent." Commander Carmine tented his fingers. "I will have Flavia forward you the coordinates to Mauw and the file we have on The Bastent. I have heard very good things about you Roxy, I can see a bright future for you with The PRC."

"Thank you, Seth. I appreciate the confidence you

have in me."

Roxy rose and smoothed the palms of her sweaty hands down along the thighs of her pencil skirt. She glanced up to find the Commander had moved closer. *Was he checking her out?*

Roxy cleared her throat to break the tension. "Any special instructions that you have for me?"

He reached down to pick up the drink he had poured earlier, threw it back, his throat working as he swallowed the amber liquid. Sweat glistened on his forehead.

"Just get the job done."

"And for clarification, this leader of The Bastent… how do you…?"

"Dead or alive Roxy." His face spread into a sinuous smile. "But preferably dead."

CHAPTER SEVEN

Roxy decided to walk the ten blocks from the business district to the Chaffey Building and the offices of Buckles & Associates. She grabbed an order of onion bhajis from a street vendor and ate as she strolled. Having missed out on breakfast, she was starving.

By the time she arrived back on her own turf, her feet were sore but her mind was clear.

It was unusually quiet when she let herself into the office. She glanced at the time and was surprised to see that the afternoon had crept up on her. Suki was likely out for lunch. Wearily she removed her heels and limped towards her inner sanctum. She sank into her chair with an audible groan of relief.

An eerie sense of calm had come over Roxy the moment she had learned that Commander Carmine was sending her to Mauw. Suddenly everything she had learned as of late made sense. She thought back to the information she had gleaned from the Witchlet Verbena before she'd exterminated her, and felt a tiny twinge of guilt for having gone back on her word.

River Lynx and Sam Sparrow were working together; Roxy was absolutely certain now. It was all coming together. And they had to be stopped.

Roxy would leave for Mauw within the hour.

She was about to kill two birds with one stone.

***

Her mood matched the gloom of the sky outside her window. Thunder grumbled in the distance.

Roxy wasn't very good at goodbyes, even the thought of them, so she busied herself: a mediocre distraction. Within a few minutes she had arranged passage on a cargo-carrier out of Aurora that evening, calling in a favor to keep her name off the official manifest.

She would leave the Zip Ship behind this time. Flight plans meant she could be tracked and she saw no reason to give warning that she was on the way.

Her wristlet beeped: a message from Commander Carmine's assistant Flavia as promised. Detailed dossiers on River Lynx and The Bastent were attached. She would read those on the trip. And then there was her contract. *That* she would read now. Roxy gave a low whistle at the payout she was due upon completion of her mission. That would buy a *lot* of sushi. A non-disclosure clause near the end spelled out in no uncertain terms that no one was to be made aware of the nature of her travels. Roxy hated keeping things from Suki but this time it would be a necessary evil.

From the closet she retrieved a change of clothes – she wouldn't be caught without one again – and quickly shrugged out of the blouse and skirt she had worn to The PRC meeting. Slim fitting dark pants, black shirt and jacket replaced them. She hauled on worn combat boots. In front of a mirror, she slicked back her short bouncy curls with gel until they were smooth against her head, and with a precision born of practice, lined her eyes with thick kohl and traded her signature bright red lipstick for a slash of deep maroon.

Roxy stared at herself for a moment, stiffened her shoulders like a good soldier. She grabbed her Go Bag and stepped out of the room, closing the door softly as she turned.

"Roxy!"

Roxy jumped. Suki had returned from lunch. "Shit, you scared me."

"You look…" Suki trailed off as she took in Roxy's changed appearance.

"I believe the word you are searching for is *delicious*." Roxy smirked.

"Wait." Suki knitted her brow, her eyes roving to the travel bag that Roxy held in her hand. "Were you leaving without saying goodbye?"

"You know I'm not good with this stuff Suki," Roxy replied, bravado gone.

"You were going to send me a Holo-Gram once you were in the air, weren't you?"

"Maybe." Roxy grimaced. Sometimes she wished Suki didn't know her quite so well.

"You don't have to do this Roxy. It's been ten years since Sparrow went AWOL. He's kept his head down. Maybe we should just leave the past where it belongs – in the past."

Ignoring Suki's plea, Roxy leaned over to place a lingering kiss on her forehead. "Remember what we used to say to each other, back at the academy, before we left on our practice missions?"

Suki snorted. "You were the one who came up with that particular gem. And *you* were the only one who ever used it. But I remember." She paused. "How long do you think you'll be gone?"

Roxy reached down and grabbed her bag. She walked to the automatic doors and stood in front them, frozen.

"Roxy?"

Roxy shook her head once, plastered on a cocky grin and glanced back over her shoulder: "Goodbye, don't cry, you'll see me soon!"

Suki groaned. "Is that a promise?"

Roxy hurried through the door before Suki had a chance to ask any more questions.

For once in her life, Roxy didn't have the answers.

***

She slipped aboard The Orbiter 3000 under cover of darkness, a wink and a nod from the porter as he unlocked the cargo hold and walked away whistling. Roxy grabbed a pile of old netting and made herself comfortable between a crate of mangolo fruit and a stack of pallets containing automatic solar trackers.

She lay back against the makeshift bed, duffle beneath her head, and scrolled through the files Flavia had sent. The report consisted mostly of third-party information and tips from shady informants. There was no solid evidence that Roxy could see. She frowned. She'd expected more. The Mauwian's were, in general, a peaceful species. There had never been a reason to visit their planet until now and they rarely, if ever, travelled outside their own. Roxy couldn't help but wonder why the Mauwian's would all of a sudden turn hostile and instigate war.

Sparrow's influence no doubt, Roxy sneered.

She yawned, her eyes heavy from reading the files in the dim light. It had been a long day. She felt the vibrations of the motors as they revved up to lift the ship from its moorings and before long, the gentle rhythmic sway of open space became a soothing lullaby and Roxy succumbed to sleep.

CHAPTER EIGHT

A heavy thump roused Roxy from her slumber. The ship had docked on Mauw. She blinked several times, driving the sleep from her eyes. She grabbed a PWR Protein Delite™ from her bag – matcha flavor this time – and ate it quickly, needing the burst of energy. She slipped the straps of her bag over her shoulders and then lingered in the shadows near the door of the cargo hold, waiting for the signal.

Three sharp raps on the door. Roxy would have mere seconds to leave the ship and find cover. Being caught as a stowaway was not an option. She detected the low whine of the gears as the door eased open and then she was out.

She ran in a low crouch and did not looking back. The sound of blood rushing and the frantic pounding of her heart was all she heard. She plunged into the gloom of a thicket of trees, dodging branches that whipped at her face as she ran. She stopped only when she could no longer see the lights of the spaceport behind her. She threw herself at the base of a large sequoia hybrid, her breath rasping loudly.

She glanced at her wristlet. No time to rest. Suntwin was rising and she still needed to do recon.

Roxy scrambled to her feet and looked for a place to secret her bag. Her eyes alighted on a natural indentation near the roots of the sequoia. She brushed away dirt and detritus and grunted in satisfaction. The opening was large enough to stuff the bag inside. She kicked leaves and twigs in front of it and stood back. It would have to do. She wiped her dirty hands on her pants and set off at a steady pace. If she remembered correctly, from the brief glance she had gotten as she left the cargo ship, there were lights to the North. Lights meant civilization.

She had gone no more than a few yards when she heard the unmistakable sound of a twig snapping beneath a foot. She slid behind a tree and became still.

"'Ello there," came a friendly voice. "Would you please come out from behind that tree? There are many of us I am afraid. I believe on your planet they say, 'you are surrounded?'"

"Dammit," Roxy muttered.

"Please do not be alarmed. We will not hurt you."

Roxy took a deep breath and stepped out from her hiding place. Any words she might have said died in her throat. Before her, in the low light of dawn, was the most stunning creature she had ever seen. Tall and covered in sleek ginger fur, festooned in khaki shorts and shirt, the Mauwian grinned at her, displaying tiny sharp teeth. Cerulean feline eyes winked at her from beneath the brim of a matching khaki beret.

"Ello." Their voice was gravelly but amiable. "My friends and I would appreciate it if you would come with us. I will walk towards you slowly and then I will take your arm."

The Mauwian seemed to be waiting for her consent.

Roxy gave a curt nod. They approached her calmly. "I am Bareen. It would be my pleasure to escort you to meet our sovereign."

Roxy's lips thinned with fury.

She'd been set up.

From behind, and to either side of Roxy, smaller but similarly dressed felines appeared. One, striped with long fur, waved cheerfully.

Bareen gently took Roxy's hand and placed it in the crook of their elbow. Arm in arm, they strolled out of the forest and along a well trodden dirt path, the other Mauwian's chattering and laughing behind them. Bareen's arm was soft and warm.

"River will be very pleased to meet you," Bareen murmured, patting Roxy's hand. "They have heard many good things about you."

It was the oddest capture Roxy had ever experienced.

The dirt path wound a circuitous route that stretched on for miles. Suntwin had reached its zenith in the sky by the time they emerged into a lush green meadow. The smaller Mauwian's dropped to all fours and loped through the grass, chasing each other, their tails high above their backs.

Bareen chuckled indulgently at their antics. "Kittens."

Roxy kept her mouth shut.

Just beyond the meadow lay a large cluster of modern wooden buildings. High above those, in the sturdy branches of the sequoia hybrids, were hundreds of tree houses. Homes, Roxy realized, taking note of a multitude of tiny faces that peered at her through the windows. Some of the treehouses were connected by large patios, others by enormous branches – both scored deeply with scratch marks and gouges. Vibrant green foliage grew unchecked on and around the houses, providing natural shade but also allowing brilliant light to filter through.

Roxy could see several fully grown Mauwian's luxuriating in the Suntwin's rays, one lay curled up on a branch nose to tail. Roxy could hear them snoring, despite the distance.

Bareen corralled her towards the largest of the low structures and Roxy reluctantly dragged her gaze away. It was a utilitarian building; two windows and a door, a small deck ran the length of the front and was home to a multitude of lush potted plants that Roxy quickly identified as Nepeta Cataria or, in layman's terms, catnip. Roxy followed Bareen up the two steps that led to the deck, eyes roving, taking notes.

It was cool inside, a welcome relief after the long walk.

"Please wait here, River will be with you shortly. I will bring you a drink."

This was the main room of a meeting hall. Chairs

were fanned out in front of a podium, and next to that, a whiteboard was cluttered with tiny cramped hand-writing. In the corner, filing cabinets were stacked in a neat line. This must be where The Bastent gathered. Their headquarters.

"Bareen will return shortly with your drink."

Roxy jumped. She spun around, chagrined at having been snuck up on again. She was losing her touch.

"I am sorry to have startled you Ms. Buckles. Sometimes we forget that humans do not sense our approach."

So, this was River Lynx. Of average human height, with golden eyes and wearing the same khaki uni-form as the others, their Bengal coat gleamed as they approached Roxy, a paw extended in greeting. Roxy ignored it.

"I am sure you have many questions and there will come a time when I will answer those for you. You have my word. In the meantime, to alleviate your curiosity, the young porter who snuck you aboard The Orbiter… he is a friend of The Bastent."

Roxy's nostrils flared. Heads would roll if she ever made it back to Aurora.

"Please do not be angry with him Ms. Buckles. He meant well."

"What do you want from me?" Roxy burst out.

"It is not *I* that wants anything from you. Al-though I am very pleased to have you here. Please, take a seat."

"Why don't *you* take that seat and shove…"

"Roxy."

Roxy gasped and spun around. Shock rippled across her face and she felt herself go cold.

He was older and a jagged scar crossed his forehead but it was him. "It's been a long time."

And then he had the gall to smile.

White hot anger exploded in Roxy's chest and her vision blurred. She launched herself across the room, tossing chairs as she went, her hands reaching blindly for Sam Sparrow's throat.

From the corner of her eye, she saw something furry launch itself in the air. She felt the jarring impact, the nothingness of freefall and then the sharp pain as her head cracked against the timber of the podium.

There was a rush of sound, voices shouting and then… nothing.

CHAPTER NINE

The terse whispers were barely audible above the steady drum of pain that threatened to rip her skull apart but they teased her to consciousness nonetheless. She blinked the room into focus.

It was a small bedroom, sparsely furnished with roughly hewn timber walls. The bed upon which she rested took up most of the space. There was a small table next to the bed that held a glass of water and, in the corner, a tall structure that Roxy thought might be a scratching post. It contained nothing else and Roxy wondered, vaguely, if this was meant to be a holding cell. An unidentifiable though not unpleasant floral scent was heavy upon the air, drifting in through the window on a gentle breeze. Gauzy drapes had been drawn against the light; they undulated lazily in the draft. The window was really all she needed to facilitate her escape.

Roxy was lying atop a firm but comfortable mattress; a downy pillow cradled her head and a delicate pastel colored muslin blanket covered her legs; a patchwork quilt was draped across the footboard.

She struggled to rise from her prone position, her hand flying to her head, and the bandage that covered it, as starbursts flared, eclipsing her vision.

She had one hell of a headache.

The door, slightly ajar, funneled the words of whomever was speaking outside it. Their voices were soft but Roxy had heard enough to know that she was the topic of conversation. She swung her feet over the side of the bed, wincing at the fresh wave of agony that the small movement caused. She pushed through it.

Get it together, Roxy, she chided. *You've dealt with far worse than a knock to the head.*

Roxy slipped from the bed and, keeping an eye and an ear to the door, tiptoed across the room, grateful that she was still wearing her shoes. Putting those on would have taken up precious time. She cringed as a floorboard creaked. She brushed aside the curtains with a trembling hand and squinted into the mid-afternoon light. If her estimates were correct, she had been unconscious and at their mercy for several hours at least, perhaps even half the day.

Sitting gingerly on the window ledge, Roxy eased her legs through the window. Giving herself a little push, she landed softly onto the green grass below, thankful that she was being held on the ground floor. She rounded the side of the building and leaned against the back wall, breathing heavily. She swiped at the greasy sheen of sweat that coated her brow and glanced back to confirm that, this time, she had not been followed. She was in the clear.

She slipped into the heavy copse of trees beyond

and was swallowed whole.

For hours Roxy followed the signal, the tracker on her supplies sending coordinates to her wristlet, leading the way back to where she had left her bag beneath the tree. She concentrated on putting one foot in front of the other, though her limbs felt impossibly heavy and her boots like weights upon her feet. She stopped only once, leaning her forehead against the rough bark of a tree, struggling for the strength to carry on. Her bandage caught on the husk as she pushed herself upright. She ripped it off, cringing as it stuck and then tossed it aside, taking vague note that the bleeding seemed to have stopped. Small blessings.

She was desperate for rest, even more desperate for water but the thought of the bag of supplies that she had hidden beneath that sequoia kept her plodding on, even when she wanted to give up. She would never be able to forgive herself for getting busted when she had first arrived and, even more so, for having been cocky enough to leave her weapon behind before she had set out in the first place.

It had been a rookie mistake.

She would not let it happen again.

As Suntwin began its descent in the sky, Roxy broke through what seemed to be a familiar thicket of woods. Assured by the coordinates on her wristlet she made her way through the dense foliage, dodged branches, tripped over roots and snapped twigs until she reached the point from which she had started.

In the rapidly fading light, she dug frantically with bare fingers, her short nails gouging viciously into the lush earth beneath the tree. She pulled the mud-speckled bag free of its confines and with shaky, dirty hands, dug around inside.

A small cry of victory: she hauled open a sealed package and threw several blobs of *Quencher* - portable drinking water that was encased in an edible membrane - into her mouth. The relief was immediate; the liquid exploded on her tongue, drenched her parched mouth and soothed her burning throat as it went down.

Her thirst momentarily satiated, she gnawed on a strip of eggplant jerky while she gathered her things together. Using a fallen frond, she brushed the dirt back into place, hoping what she had done would look natural should anyone come searching in the area.

Sleep was not an option but she badly needed it. Sitting beneath the tree she rifled through the bag once more and exhaled joyously through her teeth as her hand brushed against the small injector pen at the bottom of her bag. She'd forgotten it was there but she was damned happy to find it. Removing the cap, Roxy slammed the auto-injector into her thigh, delivering a high dose of pain relief medication directly into the muscle. It quickly spread throughout her body bringing reprieve when it was desperately needed. The cessation of the throbbing pain in her head was nearly instantaneous and the aches and discomfort of her breakneck escape and endless run into the woods seeped away.

Feeling relatively back to normal now, or as close as she was ever going to get at present time anyways,

Roxy pushed herself to her feet and brushed the bits of dirt and broken leaves off of her clothes. Her hands were filthy. She touched her head and winced; she felt dried blood and was certain that she must be covered in blood and gore. She would never dare to use a *Quencher* to clean herself. Roxy had no idea how long she'd be on her own here and water was precious. She would have to ration.

As nice and quiet as it was here, despite the peaceful solitude of the night, she definitely could not stay where she was. It would be the first place they would check once they realized she was missing, if they hadn't already. She would not underestimate them this time.

Brain churning, tossing out different scenarios and how they might play out, she tried to formulate a plan. As far as Roxy was concerned, she was going to have to go bold or... well, there would be no going home for her.

She slipped the bag over her shoulders, tightening the straps around her chest and waist so it wouldn't bounce if she had to run and secured her weapon to her thigh in a holster for easy access if she needed it. As content as she would ever be with the plan she had made on the fly, she soldiered on, heading back in the same direction from which she had come only a short while ago.

Under the cover of darkness, she would slip back into their lair.

Only this time, she was ready for them.

Roxy had claws too.

And she damn well wasn't afraid to use them.

CHAPTER TEN

"She could not have gone far. That was quite a knock to the head."

"You don't know Roxy." Sparrow gave a long-suffering sigh.

"No, I do not." There was a pause. "Forgive me my friend, but perhaps, after all this time, neither do you."

Though she was tempted to sneak a look, Roxy stayed hidden, cloaked in shadows; eavesdropping. The pain in her skull had lessened to a dull throb but she seethed with anger. It was something she knew she had to get under control. She would need a clear head for what was to come.

There was a rustle above her - someone was standing at the window. They pushed aside the drapery; a glimpse of dark calloused hands on the sill told Roxy it was Sparrow. She shrunk back, flattening herself against the exterior.

"We *have* to find her River."

"We will. Tonight, we must rest. In the morning Bereen will lead the search party. They are one of our best trackers."

"I'm going with them."

Their tone, firm: "No, you will not Sam."

There was a muttered curse and the window abruptly slammed shut. Roxy released the breath she'd been holding.

Guess Sparrow isn't the one calling the shots after all, Roxy thought, puzzled. *So, what the hell do they want with me?*

She waited until the lights in the room were extinguished and then crept back to the shelter of the trees behind the meeting hall. Things were quiet in the small Mauwian settlement; tree houses were dark and nothing but the quiet subtle sounds of night drifted through the windows high above.

Still, Roxy would maintain her vigil.

The faint sound of footsteps drifted to her ears and a dark shape paused at the periphery of the forest. *Sparrow.* He began walking in the opposite direction of the village. Roxy waited a few beats, then followed, keeping close to the treeline, her dark clothes blending in with the night.

After hiking a short distance, a separate dwelling loomed out of nowhere, all on its own. Sparrow climbed a short ladder and entered a hut that rested on the lower branches of another massive sequoia. It was octagonal like the other tree houses she had observed but smaller: big enough for just one man. She heard muffled sounds issuing from inside and then, a few minutes later he re-emerged, drink in hand and leaned a hip against the railing that surrounded the platform of the house. He rubbed absently at the scar on his forehead.

He looked a little worse for the wear she had to admit, his hair was longer now; there were several days of bristly growth on his face and his clothes were rumpled and sweat-stained. Roxy felt a twinge of something that might have been pity. This was a different Sam Sparrow than the one she had known. How the mighty had fallen. He looked... defeated.

No. Roxy shook herself mentally. Now was not the time for sentimentalities. She needed to focus on what she had come here to do. Once that was sorted, she would do the job The Planetary Regulation Committee had hired her for. She'd found herself rather underwhelmed by River Lynx, despite their reputation as a tyrant and leader of a fascist regime. Roxy expected they could be disposed of with very little effort on her part, a quick slice of a blade; up close and personal.

She watched from the shadows as Sam tossed back his drink and with a deep sigh that was audible even from the distance that separated them, he went back inside. She would bide her time. He'd have to sleep eventually.

Afraid that the light from her wristlet might alert someone to her position, Roxy sat in the shadows with nothing but her dark thoughts to keep her company:

And she was right back there. It was immediately after the explosion. Smoke, dust and the incessant keening of an alarm filled the burning air. She staggered through the rubble, trying to blink dirt and blood out of her eyes. She heard shouting, crying and then suddenly realized that it was her: she was screaming their names, struggling to be heard above the cacophony of disaster.

"Ma'am? Ma'am are you alright? Do you need help?"

The voice came from behind her, muffled. Her ears still rang from the blast. She'd been one of the lucky ones, if you could call it luck: she'd been on the lower levels, about to exit the building, when the blast hit and she had been able to drag herself free.

"My friends! You have to help them!"

"Were they down here with you?" The man in the high-tech rescue gear had to yell to be heard above the whir of rescue helicopters over head and the sirens of emergency vehicles on the ground.

"No... no they were on the 180th floor."

The look on his face told her all that she needed to know.

Well over an hour passed while Roxy remained lost in her memories. She was stiff from sitting in the same spot for so long; she stretched and flexed and emerged from hiding with renewed focus and determination. The time had come. She crept up the ladder, kept her body low to the floor and effected an army crawl along the platform. She would avoid the front door in case it was secured. The windows had been left open though, allowing a balmy breeze to circulate the hut. Roxy risked a glimpse inside. She couldn't help as a small gasp of surprise escaped her lips. Roxy had expected a sparse hideout at best, a place to hunker down and lay low for a while before moving on again, but... Sam had made a *home* here. There was even a vase of flowers on the kitchen table.

Roxy inched around to the next window. A low lamp had been left on in the far corner, a faint blush of light illuminated the man on the bed; a simple white sheet covered his lower half and one arm was flung above his head, across a pillow. He was breathing deeply, sleeping soundly. *Of course.* Roxy averted her gaze but not before getting an eyeful of firm golden male skin.

Nothing you haven't seen before Roxy, she scolded. *Stop stalling.*

She threw one leg through the opening, easing herself across the sill. The floor beneath her boot creaked and she froze, her heart in her throat. Sparrow stirred and the sheet slipped, perching precariously low across his hips. But he did not wake. Roxy sent up a silent prayer of thanks and swung the rest of her body inside. She knelt and pulled a short knife from her boot and stealthily crossed the room.

When Sparrow's eyes popped open, he didn't seem all that surprised to find Roxy straddling him, the sharp edge of her karambit pressing against his throat. He searched her eyes and an expression of something akin to sadness flickered across his face; it happened so quickly that Roxy wondered if perhaps she had imagined it. It was promptly replaced by calm indifference.

Roxy defiantly held his gaze. She'd waited a long time for this moment and the thrill of it thrummed through her veins.

"Any last words Sparrow?" Roxy whispered.

"Not really," Sam drawled. "Only I seem to recall that the last time you were in this position, it was a lot more enjoyable for the both of us."

A lazy grin spread across his face and Roxy's eyes narrowed. With one judiciously aimed blow to the temple, Sparrow was out cold. Roxy sat back and let loose with a string of profanity she was sure would have made a sailor-bot blush.

Dammit. Now she would have to wait until he came to. Despite her reputation, she wasn't the type who would slit the throat of an unconscious man. Even scum like Sam Sparrow.

Roxy began a thorough search the house. She pulled contents from drawers, rummaged through cupboards and poked through the cedar chest at the foot of the bed. Blankets, books and papers; she brought up short when she hauled out a framed photograph. It was Sam... and Roxy. She was looking into the camera, her arm thrown around his shoulders, a wide grin on her face. And Sam. Well, Sam was looking at her. They looked happy. In love.

She quickly jammed the frame back beneath the blankets and closed the lid of the chest. More rattled at the discovery than she cared to admit, and not having found anything of worth, she grabbed the sheet from the bed and, using her knife, sliced it into serviceable strips. With practiced movements - ignoring the now naked fugitive on the bed - Roxy tied Sam's wrists and ankles tightly to the bedframe. She dragged a chair in from the other room and sat next to the bed; her anger a slow simmer just below the surface.

Okay. She would wait, get some answers from him first.

Because she sure had a lot of fucking questions.

And *then* she'd kill him.

CHAPTER ELEVEN

Boots resting on a bedside table, feet crossed at the ankles, Roxy was flipping nonchalantly through the pages of a book on deep space flora, when Sparrow began to slowly regain consciousness. A smirk played across her lips. She watched from the corner of her eye as he examined the makeshift restraints. He glared at her as she continued to flick through the pages.

"That was my best sheet, Roxy."

Roxy rolled her eyes and tossed the book to one side. "You're lucky it was just the sheet."

He grimaced. "Untie me."

"No."

He struggled, yanked on the bindings, but Roxy knew she had tied a damned good knot – he wasn't going anywhere, and his struggles were only making them tighter. She could see his frustration was mounting and a pleasant shiver of satisfaction coursed through her. She was in charge now.

"Could you at least throw a blanket on me then?"

Hand on her hip, Roxy raised an eyebrow in mock disappointment. "Why Sam Sparrow, have you gone and turned shy?"

"You don't have to be so goddamned smug you know."

"Why shouldn't I?" Roxy growled, giving him a glimpse of her anger. "I have you exactly where I want you."

"Naked and tied up in bed?" Sam chucked, his eyes raking over Roxy. "Darlin' all you had to do was ask."

Roxy swore in frustration and stomped from the room, Sam's throaty laughter following close behind her. She grabbed a checkered throw blanket from the back of a chair and returned to toss it hastily across the lower half of his body.

"What exactly do you have to laugh about? I could kill you right here and right now without absolutely any remorse."

"Why haven't you then?"

Roxy blinked. "I… I have questions."

"Don't we all." He muttered under his breath then, "Listen, Roxy, I'm not the person you seem to think I am."

Roxy laughed mirthlessly. "I thought I knew who you were but that's not the real Sam Sparrow at all."

"I'm telling you the truth," Sam interjected. "I have been all along. I had *nothing* to do with that explosion. I would never…" He trailed off and shook his head. "I would never hurt anyone like that."

Roxy glared at him in disgust. "You were arrested. Convicted in absentia. Guilty as charged."

"I am innocent."

"Yeah, they all say that." Roxy rolled her eyes.

"Come on Roxy," Sam bellowed. "You *know* me. How could you ever think…? I would never put the people I love in danger like that. Not Suki… and definitely not you."

"Don't you dare talk about love." Roxy shouted back. "Suki almost died, spent *months* in hospital. Months of pain and surgeries and physical therapy. That is on *your* head. I *never* knew you."

Roxy glared at him, struggled to control her breathing. The pounding in her temples amplified. She turned away; head bowed.

"Look at me, please. It was a set up Roxy." Sam tried to catch her gaze, his eyes pleading. "They needed a scape goat and I was the perfect choice. Who would believe me, some cocky fly-guy fresh out of the Academy who was already butting heads, over the word of the Commander of The PRC?"

Roxy gaped. "Are you trying to say Commander Carmine lied? That he *framed* you? Wow. You are even crazier than I thought."

"I am not crazy," Sam erupted. "Why won't you believe me. I did not lie."

"Fine then," Roxy shrugged her shoulders, calling his bluff. "Prove it."

Sam looked defeated. "What about my word? That used to be enough for you."

"Innocent men don't run."

He looked at her, his eyes pleading for understanding. "I had no choice. They would have executed me if I'd stayed."

Roxy stood, nodding in agreement. "And rightfully so."

"Roxy, please…"

She crossed her arms, remained silent.

Sam swore under his breath. "We, Rover and I and The Bastent, plan on exposing The Commander and his flunkies at The PRC for what they truly are. Something is coming Roxy. Something big. And he's behind the whole damned thing."

"Or so you say."

"A long extinct species suddenly reappearing… Earthside of all places and a LanQuid of all things. Look at all those Witchlet kidnappings; you don't think The PRC keeps eyes on those things? Why haven't they put a stop to it? I think you know why. Because it benefits them. You don't even know the half of it. The things they've done and continue to do."

"Why would Seth have sent me *here* then?"

"Oh, it's *Seth* now, is it?" Sam gave a short bark of laughter. "Because he's getting scared. He's finally realizing just how close we are to taking him down. And he knows all about your vendetta. He's using you to get rid of me and River. Once we're gone, The Bastent will collapse and he can go right back to doing whatever the hell he wants."

"That's ludicrous." Roxy scoffed, "Commander Carmine wouldn't have even known you were here."

"No? For fuck's sake Roxy, when did you become such a goddamned sheep? Seth Carmine is the one who helped me escape."

Roxy gasped. "Will you stop at no lengths to…"

"He threw me the keys to a PRC Zip," Sam continued, raising his voice to be heard. "Told me to run. It was all a part of his plan. He's known where I've been this whole time. You can ask River. They granted me asylum on Mauw and I've been here ever since. You're smart. Think about it."

Roxy gnawed on her bottom lip and then appeared to reach a decision. She bent to retrieve the karambit from her boot. Sam collapsed back against the pillows, frustrated, and sighed in defeat. Roxy stood over him, the light from the lamp in the corner glinted wickedly along the blade as she ran her thumb across its edge.

"You know what Sam; I don't like liars." She paused and studied his face, "But I also don't like being someone's bitch."

She leaned over and began to slice through his restraints.

"Take me to River."

CHAPTER TWELVE

A match flared in the darkness and the sweet scent of herbs permeated the air.

"Did you know Roxy Buckles, that a Mauwian's olfactory sense is thirty times better than that of a human? And that despite this delightful nip that I am partaking of, I can still smell you there?"

"Oh yeah?" Roxy snarked. "And what do I smell like?"

River inhaled deeply, then on an exhalation of smoke: "Melons."

Sam coughed to cover a laugh and Roxy glared at him in the gloom.

River Lynx chuckled. "It is safe to approach. I will not harm you Ms. Buckles. You have my word. As long as I have yours that you will not use that knife on Sam."

"Maybe you should have mentioned that to your friend from earlier," Roxy returned, wincing. The tender spot at her hairline and the still present headache were a not so pleasant reminder of the encounter.

"I am deeply sorry that you were injured Ms.

Buckles. I have had a word with Kashmir and they will be scooping litter for months to make amends. They are young and were trying to protect Sam."

Roxy rolled her eyes. *Sam, Sam, Sam.* "Not only harbouring but protecting a known fugitive?"

River Lynx stepped into the pool of light that bled from the windows of the large hut behind them. A tendril of smoke curled around their head and Roxy could see the flash of shrewd feline eyes as they assessed her.

"You have much to learn Ms. Buckles."

"Is that right?" Roxy nudged Sam forward with an elbow. "Perhaps you'd care to enlighten me then," she added dryly, her words dripping with skepticism.

"I would be delighted." River gestured with the sweep of a paw for Roxy and Sam to follow, dropping the end of their still smoldering cigarette into a small jar of liquid on the balcony of the hut. "But first, I will need you to sheath your weapon."

Roxy hesitated. Trust was not something that came easily to her. *Well, they've already had multiple opportunities to kill you if they really wanted to*, she reassured herself. She gave a curt nod and slipped the knife back into her boot, comforted by the fact that it was easily accessible if she needed it. Sam followed River into the dwelling, with Roxy close behind.

River's home was larger than Sam's by half. Built in book cases lined the walls, overloaded with a haphazard assortment of scientific journals and large volumes of fiction, it looked ready to collapse; a large basket of yarn was filled to overflow in one corner. The rooms were neat and tidy with large overstuffed furniture. Throw blankets and large pillows were in abundance and lush green plants covered every available surface.

"Please take a seat. May I get you a drink?" River offered, the epitome of the perfect host as they poured themselves a saucer of cream. "I have herbal tea, or ice water if you'd prefer."

Sam lowered himself onto a bench. "Water would be great, thanks River."

Roxy crossed her arms and glared at the both of them.

"As you wish Ms. Buckles."

The conversation that followed left Roxy reeling. She crossed the room and collapsed into a chair.

Ten years of her life – she'd been living a lie.

Sam sat quietly, watching Roxy intently as she absorbed the news. River presented their case - cold hard facts and evidence that Roxy could not ignore. The most damning of all, grainy footage obtained from the damaged front-end camera of the PRC Zip Ship as Sparrow flew away from Aurora for the final time – there was Commander Seth Carmine standing on the tarmac, watching... completely and utterly fine. No bruises, no cuts or contusions, nothing to indicate a severe concussion; no blood from the brutal beating he had claimed Sparrow had inflicted on him.

River spoke passionately but not fanatically; they were articulate and well informed and remarkably calm for someone who had just dropped the emotional equivalent of an atomic bomb.

"The Commander is hungry, his appetite for power continues to grow. Do you understand Roxy Buckles?" River implored. "If we do not take him down, if we do not put a stop to this, many more innocents will suffer and die."

Roxy nodded, then stood and stepped through the door of the hut, her breathing ragged as she leaned over the railing of the balcony, trying to blink away the shadows that encroached at the edge of her vision. The familiar burden of guilt and regret weighed heavy on her shoulders.

She had been presented with irrefutable proof that Commander Carmine was corrupt.

And that Sam Sparrow was innocent.

She desperately needed to speak with Suki and cursed at the uselessness of her wristlet and its inability to communicate at this distance. Suki was her connection to the real world, to home, and without that tether, she felt adrift and alone.

Roxy heard the soft pad of paws approach her from behind. River Lynx joined her at the balcony and stood in quiet contemplation.

"What?" Roxy barked, finally, when the silence became too loud.

"I understand you are in turmoil, Ms. Buckles and I am sympathetic to your pain. But now I want you to imagine how Sam has felt for the past ten years." They paused, watching Roxy with judicious eyes. "I have had Kashmir prepare a space for you for the night. I will take you there. You should rest."

"I'll show her the way River," Sam eased himself through the doorway of the hut.

Roxy put her head down and threw her walls up. A terse, whispered conversation between River and Sam lasted less than a minute and then Roxy and Sam were alone.

"Well, you *were* looking for a bad guy to kill." Sam shrugged, his attempt at a joke to ease the tension falling flat. "It's just a different guy now."

Roxy took a calming breath. "When's the next cargo ship out of here? I need to get back to Aurora and fix this mess."

Sam cleared his throat. "We're all going. We still have the PRC Zip Ship in dry dock. It's not as modern as the new ones but I repaired it as best I could, it'll get us there."

Roxy finally looked at Sam. "You'll be arrested on sight."

"I'll have to take the risk. I won't let you and River fight this alone."

"I can handle it."

"I'm not saying you can't but goddamn it, Roxy, that man took everything from me. I *need* to do this."

Roxy pushed past Sam and down the steps of the treehouse. She set off at a brisk pace with no particular destination in mind, just a desire to put distance between herself and the past.

"Roxy! Wait up." Sam called to her from across the clearing.

Her footsteps slowed - she owed him that much she decided - and Sam jogged up beside her.

"There is just one more thing we need to discuss."

"What could we possibly have left to talk about?" Roxy demanded, frowning.

Sam regarded her with a mixture of sadness and longing, "us."

"There is no *us* Sam."

"Roxy…"

"No."

He sighed. "You've heard River out. At the very least, let me tell you my side of the story, in my own words. Please."

"Okay, Sam," she took a deep breath. This was harder than she would have imagined it being. "I guess it's time. I'm listening."

CHAPTER THIRTEEN

Sam flattened himself against the wall, the chill of the brick exterior penetrating easily through the thin white fabric of the threadbare shirt that served as part of his prison garb. He gasped for air, his chest heaving; those daily runs on the treadmill having done very little to prepare him for the eventuality of long distance running and dodging the law. Sweat dripped into his eyes; he swiped a trembling hand across his forehead surprised to see it come away stained with blood. The prison guard hadn't gone down without a fight that was for sure.

He quickly considered his options.

Well, he could turn himself in.

He stifled a short bark of laughter.

Fuck no, that wasn't happening. Not when he had worked so hard to get away.

So, there was only one choice left: he would have to keep running until he was able to prove his innocence. All he had to do now was make it off Aurora alive, dodging both the Gendarme and the wrath of the very people he had thought were his friends…

who he thought would always stick by his side. The betrayal left a bitter taste on his tongue. No, he had to get out of here and get out quick. Along the way he would have to avoid all the check points he was sure had been set up by now, the roadblocks and the air patrols who'd all be on the lookout for him.

He'd bet money they'd been given the order to apprehend at all costs.

Dead or alive.

But somehow, before undertaking all of that, he had to remove the tracking device they'd implanted in his forearm. He'd never make it otherwise.

Piece of cake, he thought ruefully.

He inched along the wall, desperately seeking cover, knowing he had to act quickly before they caught up to him. Quietly gaining access to a building would be ideal. The warehouse district in which he currently stood was rife with abandoned business fronts and condemned buildings. This was one of them, Sam was sure, the one he currently leaned against – the burned-out vehicle in the parking lot was as good an indication as any. As he rounded the corner at the back of the building, he lowered to a crouch preparing for what might be an ambush on the other side. Relief weakened his knees – there was nothing, no one in sight. He'd given them the slip.

For now.

Ah but there *was* a door. Sam worried about the noise he was about to make but considered it a small price to pay. He threw his full weight against the door, grunting with the effort, the tendons in his neck straining. He gave a soft cry of triumph when the flimsy lock gave way and the door swung inwards. Success.

It was dark and dank inside the building but it was quiet and it was empty. Refuge. Sam kicked his way through detritus and debris that had been left behind when the owners had hauled up stakes, and the trash left behind by squatters and hoodlums who'd been looking for a place to party or do drugs. Everything was coated in a thick layer of dust and grime and things Sam didn't even want to think about.

Across the wide expanse of the warehouse, Sam spotted what was probably once an office space; a hidey hole for the boss where he could keep an eye on his employees. The door was angled at a heavy lean; Sam pushed it back against the wall, one rusted hinge squawking in protest. He took stock of the meager furnishings inside: a wooden desk, a swivel chair, a filing cabinet and a shelf. All sagging or rusted. The heavy smell of mildew assaulted his nose.

Sam pushed the chair to one side dislodging a torrent of mouse droppings from a hole in the stuff. He shuddered but a search of this room was essential. The desk drawers were warped with age and water damage and gave protest when he tried to open them. But Sam was persistent. With a hideous screech the drawer released and spilled forth its contents. Nothing more than some faded receipts and a letter opener. He continued his exploration. Inside the larger bottom drawer: a half bottle of amber liquid and a small tumbler. Sam gave the bottle a sniff – definitely alcohol. The letter opener he'd found in the first drawer would have to do; he didn't have many other options.

He splashed the booze onto the letter opener, took a couple of deep breaths and with prodding fingers located the small lump on his forearm that indicated the injection site of his remote tracking device. He closed his eyes, and steeled himself. Ready as he would ever be, he placed the pointed edge of the letter opener against his bronzed skin and then he pushed as hard as he could, drawing it down and across his flesh. His vision narrowed to a point. He closed his eyes. Starbursts exploded behind his eyelids and he fought for control.

He was panting heavily, sweat beading on his upper lip and forehead, staining the underarms of his shirt, by the time he'd dug the small device out of his flesh. Waves of darkness threatened to pull him under but he gritted his teeth against the seduction of oblivion. He threw the capsule sized device to the floor and stomped on it with his combat boot, smashing it to bits.

Foregoing the dusty drinking glass Sam pounded back the liquid in the bottle, swallowing convulsively until it ran dry. His eyes watered and he coughed. He wondered how old the drink had been but figured that it was probably the least of his worries today. He ripped a sleeve off his shirt and bound it clumsily around the gaping wound in his arm. Red slowly seeped into the makeshift bandage. He probably needed stitches but at least at least now he was flying under the radar.

He took a shuddering breath.

Now he had to get the hell out of dodge.

CHAPTER FOURTEEN

A quick search of the warehouse turned up a motheaten peacoat, a baseball cap that had seen better days and an old Swiss Army knife that was better than no weapon at all. Sam eased the coat over his injured arm, pulled the hat low on his head and slipped the new found weapon into a pocket for easy access. He scanned the area outside the building as he slipped through the door and back into the light of day. He blinked; his eyes slow to adjust to the change from dim and dank to Suntwin.

He had no idea where to go. With a pang, he thought of Roxy but quickly dismissed the idea. Their meeting at the prison hadn't gone as he had envisioned. In his head he'd imagined tears, Roxy insisting he'd be freed and then her promise to prove him innocent, maybe even just a hug. Instead, the guards had had to hold her back from strangling him with her bare hands. He was still in shock that she could believe he would do such a thing. He thought of Peter, Erik, Johanna, Mel, Dr. Kristina, Lizzie and so many others... gone in the blink of an eye. And

Suki. He hadn't been permitted to visit her at the hospital. From what he had been told, she wouldn't have known he was there anyways.

The shock waves of the bomb had spread out and up. Suki had been a mere three floors above the center of the blast. It was a miracle she had survived at all. Her saving grace – she'd been in a class demonstrating the use of tactical gear and had been suited up in full regalia. If not for the helmet…

Everyone else in that room had died that day.

They'd shown Sam the photos of the aftermath during his interrogation; the mangled bodies, the severed limbs, the blood and brick, the dust and debris. Suki covered in bandages, tubes and wires everywhere, surrounded by machines keeping her alive. If they hadn't told him that it was Suki there in that hospital bed, he would have never believed it.

Those images would haunt Sam until his dying day.

He eased himself around the corner of the building. All clear. He'd have to sprint across the wide-open expanse of the parking lot to make it to one of the other warehouses. Behind that was a highway – he might be able to hitch a ride or sneak onto a Transport Barge.

The blow above his left ear sent Sam reeling. He dropped to the ground like an anvil, the rush of blood roared in his ears.

He had little time to get his bearings, the shiny tips of expensive crocator shoes entered the periphery of his vision and then everything went hazy as his tenuous grip on consciousness slowly began to ebb away.

***

It was cold when he awoke, face down on the freezing asphalt. He raised his hand, touched his fingers tentatively to the space behind that throbbed in time with his heartbeat. It came away slick with blood. He groaned.

"Oh good, you're awake. I thought I was going to have to throw a bucket of ice water on you."

The familiar voice crashed into Sam as he opened his eyes. His vision swam but suddenly he was all too aware of where he was…. and just who was talking to him.

"Well come on then. We don't have much time. Very clever removing that tracking device Sparrow, but that's going to leave a nasty scar you know."

Commander Seth Carmine's mellifluous tones were laced with humor, but underneath Sam could sense something cold and reptilian in the man. Seth Carmine was the type that would eat his own young. Or toss them at monsters without looking back, just so he could get away.

Sam stumbled to his feet. He swayed, took deep breaths as he struggled to regain his balance.

"I suppose you're wondering why you're here?" Carmine remarked, quirking an eyebrow as he casually examined his fingernails.

Standing beneath the portico of the Zip-Ship launch at The PRC high-rise Sam did indeed wonder why he was there and why he was not immediately sent back to lockup or why he hadn't found himself on a one-way, all expenses paid trip to Brig-5.

"You could say that," Sam drawled slowly.

Carmine tossed something in Sam's direction. He grabbed it in mid-air before it could smack him in the face.

"Zip keys?" Sam questioned, incredulous as he stared down at the item in his hand. "What the fuck is going on here?"

"Go," Carmine said.

Sam shook his head, bewildered. He stayed stock still, waiting for the catch.

"Did I stutter?" Carmine burst out. "God damn it Sparrow. Go. Get out of here right now. The Zip is fuelled and ready to go."

Sam's jaw dropped.

Carmine jerked his chin in the direction of the Zip. "Now."

Sam studied him for a moment, calculated his chances if he didn't jump at this opportunity. This could give him time to prove his innocence. And doing so should be a piece of cake with the Commander of The PRC on his side. With a sudden burst of clarity, he realized exactly where he needed to go. It would be safe, quiet, and impartial. They would help him there.

Sam ran for the Zip. He quickly did pre-flight checks. The ship had just enough fuel to get him where he needed to go. With the flick of a few buttons, Sam was airborne. As the vessel began to gain altitude Sam hovered just above the tarmac. He locked eyes with Carmine and held his gaze. Before the Zip banked, he saw the Commander casually wave, his blazer flapping in the downward breeze created by the ship.

For some reason, Sam could not bring himself to wave back.

***

There was an uneasy silence when Sam finished speaking. His voice had grown hoarse near the end; it had been a long time since he had talked this much. Roxy had listened respectfully, for once not interjecting or interrupting to ask questions.

Sam searched her face for a hint of what she might be thinking.

"You don't believe me," he finally murmured, his expression bleak.

"I'm sorry Sam."

The breath he'd been holding spilled out of him in a rush. "It's okay Roxy. I understand. I can't expect you to… "

"No Sam, I mean I'm sorry for everything. I do believe you. And now, I have to go and make things right."

CHAPTER FIFTEEN

There had been a tense sort of calm inside the Zip for the first half of the jaunt back to Aurora. With each of the three occupants lost in their own thoughts, small talk and any sort of conversation had been off the table. At one point, Sam had fallen asleep, lulled by the rocking of the ship and what had probably been ten years of restless sleep.

Slumped down in the co-pilot seat, twitching occasionally, head back and mouth open he'd begun to snore loudly - much to the chagrin of his travel companions. The raucous noise had served one purpose though, to break some of the tension between Roxy and River who had now joined together in a solidarity born of annoyance.

"I suppose it would be in poor taste to throw him off the ship?" River remarked dryly.

Roxy stifled a laugh. Though the atmosphere inside the Zip had become cordial, it still hadn't stopped River from questioning everything that Roxy did: nitpicking about her speed, alternatively suggesting she slow down and then go faster; shouting if they thought Roxy was going to hit something and using a death grip on the arms of their seat, so much so that they left claw marks. They had been a typical backseat driver the whole way from Mauw and it had chewed away at Roxy's last nerve. Their squabbling had eventually woken Sam who refused to believe he'd been snoring.

"Okay!" Roxy shouted. "Everyone just shut up and let me fly."

A blessed silence had ensued for the duration of their jaunt. Roxy let out the breath she had been holding since liftoff. Nearly there.

***

"Here. Take these." As their ascent approached, Roxy reached inside her coat and, with the quick flick of a wrist, tossed a small sealed plastic packet across the bridge to Sam. The ancient Zip Ship she was piloting did not have autopilot capabilities, she needed at least one hand on the steering gyre at all times. She'd forgotten how advanced these things had become in the past ten years, thinking of her own fleet back at Buckles & Associates.

Sam ripped into the package; two small white capsules fell into his hand. He passed one of those behind him to River, sitting in the jump seat.

"And what are these exactly?" River inquired from the back, a note of scepticism in their voice. Roxy groaned internally, steeling herself for an argument she felt certain was on the way.

"*NoTraks*. They block scanning systems and interfere with surveillance cameras and facial recognition software. It gives us a brief window of opportunity to get you into Aurora undetected. Should last long enough to get you inside my condo. I have my own set of security features there so you'll be safe. Take them now so they have time to kick in."

Sam raised an eyebrow. "I didn't know this existed. I guess there are a lot of things I don't know about now." He was right. Ten years was a long time and Aurora had advanced by leaps and bounds in that time.

"Well, they aren't easy to come by," Roxy admitted cagily, "but I know some people."

"I bet you do," River murmured.

Roxy glanced back over her shoulder. Surprised, she watched as River tossed the capsule into their mouth, swallowing without further complaint. It was the first real indication of trust Roxy had gotten from the Mauwian. She felt some of the tension seep from her shoulders.

"We're about fifteen minutes out." Roxy assessed the instruments that were lit up in front of her and flipped a switch; a gridded map illuminated on a screen, coordinates flashing in red. "I'm heading straight for my office building. We can park the Zip in the garage. I need to speak with Suki first. She'll be worried."

"Look, I've been thinking Roxy," Sam hesitated, then seemed to make a decision. He plunged ahead: "Perhaps it would be safer for Suki if she didn't know about this until… until its all over and done with."

"Sam is right," River agreed, leaning forward to touch his shoulder in support. "In the long run it may be better for your friend to remain ignorant to our plans. She will have plausible deniability. From what Sam has told me, Ms. Kwan has suffered enough at Carmine's hands."

Roxy bit her lip, torn. Was she being selfish, rushing to see Suki, did she simply want to assuage her guilt? As much as she hated to admit it, Roxy knew Sam and River were right. Suki had to be protected at all costs. She had suffered enough. Roxy swore loudly and leaned forward to reprogram the coordinates into the grid map, so that the flight plan ended at the condos parking garage.

"You're right. The less people we have involved the better. What Suki doesn't know can't hurt her."

She saw Sam and River exchange relieved glances. They'd been expecting a fight.

Roxy took a deep breath. "Five minutes out."

"Wow. It's certainly changed," Sam observed with a low whistle, his eyes wide with wonder as the vista of Aurora unfolded below them. The lights of the city, auspicious and grandiose reached out towards the Zip Ship welcoming them into its burnished embrace. Though Roxy did this frequently, this re-entry into Aurora was a new experience every single time. New buildings sometimes seemed to appear over night in the ever-growing capitol and she was always a little bit dazzled as her home planet came into view.

"Time has a way of doing that," Roxy remarked

after a pause. She glanced at Sam. He looked like he hadn't heard her at all, his face pressed against the window of the ship like an Earthside child, peering wide-eyed into a candy shop. She felt a twinge of guilt along with a mix of emotions she refused to acknowledge.

"Are you sure this is going to work?" Sam inquired as the Zip made its final descent. "I hate to stand by, idle, while you do all the setup work. There has to be something I can do."

"You can hang tight and try to relax. It's nothing I can't handle," Roxy insisted, as she wrestled with the gyre, vibrating in her hands as it fought the descent. "Just let me set things up with Carmine. We can't risk either of you being seen by him or any of his goons. Not right away at least. We need the element of surprise."

Sam huffed an audible sigh of frustration. "Okay, and then what will you do?"

Roxy turned to meet Sam's eyes; her face set with grim determination. "What I always do Sam. I'm going to kill the monster."

CHAPTER SIXTEEN

"Roxy Buckles! To what do I owe the pleasure?"

The warm greeting at the other end of the call poured over Roxy like molten honey and for a moment she simply enjoyed the feeling it evoked in her, the rush of calm.

"Roxy?" The voice immediately grew heavy with concern. "Everything okay?"

"Remember when you said if I ever needed your help, all I had to do was call?" She paused, uncertain whether she was doing the right thing or not. She didn't want to drag someone else into the fracas. "Well, I'm calling."

Zillo had access to a range of technology and equipment Roxy could only dream of. Buckles & Associates just didn't have the budget. Maybe, after this job, it might.

The low husky chuckle reverberated down the line. "I meant every word of it Roxy. Anything at all. What can I do for you?"

Roxy explained, briefly, the plan she had already set in motion and how he might be able to help.

"Come by my office. I've got just the thing."

Relief flooded Roxy. "I can't think you enough Zillo. I'm on my way."

***

CommsLink was located in the Warehouse District of New Cosmos. Major upgrades had been done to the area over the years and now it was booming. Zillo's company was housed in a squat non-descript brick building that backed onto the highway. A simple black and white sign hung above the main entrance. Roxy doubled checked that she had the right place and tried not to be underwhelmed. Greeted by an old manual door that had obviously not been replaced since the original construction, Roxy leaned into it, trying to push her way inside only to discover she actually needed to pull. She cringed in embarrassment as she stepped over the threshold.

Her jaw dropped.

The inside of CommsLink was in stark contrast to its outside. *They weren't wrong when they said not to judge a book by it's cover*, Roxy thought to herself as she tried to take it all in. State of the art yet stylish, the foyer dazzled. A transparent glass desk to the left of the doorway was staffed by a young woman, from Earthside if Roxy was not mistaken. She smiled at Roxy.

"We've been expecting you Ms. Buckles."

"Thank you, Bridget, I'll take it from here."

Zillo raised his hand in an eager greeting to Roxy, his voice booming across the marble floored lobby.

He embraced her enthusiastically and Roxy sank into his arms with a mixture of relief and something she couldn't quite describe.

Maybe it was hope.

Maybe it was lust.

She was all over the place these days.

Zillo made Roxy think of long nights at home and easy mornings lingering over coffee, walks along The Esplanade, holding hands, and wine by the fire; holidays and celebrations and…

Oh god. Zillo made Roxy think long term. And Roxy Buckles did not do long term. Not anymore.

And Sam. Sam made Roxy think of things she'd buried long ago, things that she had worked hard to forget. Once upon a time *he* had been her long term.

She groaned internally. Things were getting far too complicated. What had happened to the simple life she had come to enjoy? She would definitely need time to eat her feelings once this whole thing was over. An entire sheet cake and a case of beer sounded good right about now.

Zillo was dressed for his office persona. A crisp white shirt fairly shone beneath a sharp black pin-stripe suit. It hung on his shoulders as only something *that* expensive could, it hugged his biceps and stretched across his broad chest as he moved towards her. The cufflinks at his wrists were gold inlaid with black opal. But his shirt had been opened at the collar; his tie loosened; he clearly hadn't shaved that morning – possibly not even the morning before that. A smear of grease streaked across his forehead his forehead. Roxy tried unsuccessfully to smother a grin.

"What so funny?" He asked, his brow furrowing, his smile uncertain.

Roxy stepped up to him, yanked a white handkerchief from his breast pocket and leaned in close, her breath mingling with his as she gently wiped the dirt from his face.

Roxy returned the once pristine handkerchief to his pocket.

"I guess I missed a spot." Zillo blushed charmingly. "Come with me."

He grabbed her hand as though it were the most natural thing in the world and pulled her along to the glass elevator located at the center of the main foyer. Zillo waved his free hand in front of an illuminated panel and the door whooshed open.

"Daedalus Lab," Zillo spoke aloud and winked at Roxy.

"No offence Zillo because I know the crazy amount of tech you produce out of this place, but… how in the world can you do that in such a small space?"

Suddenly, the elevator dropped and Roxy gasped.

Zillo chucked. "Sorry for not telling you. I wanted to see the look on your face."

Roxy would have smacked him had she not been so busy looking at the incredible views that surrounded her. To stave off the claustrophobia of travelling underground, through what was, at times, solid rock, the elevator walls projected moving images of stunning vistas, rolling hills and ocean views. She felt Zillo squeeze her hand. His boyish enthusiasm was contagious.

Mere moments later the elevator coasted to an easy stop and the doors opened to reveal a long white, seemingly endless hallway with numbered doors on either side.

"How far down are we?" Roxy asked in a hushed tone.

"Two point five kilometers." He stated proudly. "Upstairs we have a few boardrooms and offices; I use one floor as an apartment and I stay there sometimes when I'm working and don't want to waste time going home; there's a bit of storage but, to be honest, it's mostly for show. The real magic happens down here."

Zillo pulled her along the corridor until they came to a door near the end of the hall – number 144. Zillo's handprint opened the door and the lights came on automatically as they entered. The room was larger than Roxy had expected, air conditioned to keep the temperature suitable for all the computers and hard drives. Work benches lined the walls, their contents organized chaos. Screens and touch tables filled every other available space around the room. A large antique mahogany desk had been pushed to one side near the door and was stacked high with books, papers, and electronic components. There were no chairs. *Does he ever sit down?* Roxy pondered.

Zillo gave her hand another squeeze and then released it, tugging off his tie, shrugging out of his jacket and rolling up the sleeves of his shirt.

"There. That's much better. I had a meeting this morning," he said in way of explanation and grimaced to show how little he had enjoyed the experience.

Roxy lingered near the doorway. Her hand still tingled from the contact with Zillo. She pushed the confusion that swirled within her to the back of her mind to ruminate on later and forced herself to ignore the feeling. She followed along behind Zillo as he walked to the longest table at the back of the room.

"I've been working on a little something. It's relatively new but has passed the first, second and third rounds of experimental trials in the lab. We will be ready to launch to the public soon. But you, my dear, are getting first dibs!"

With a flourish he presented a small clear patch in the palm of his hand, about the size of an old-fashioned book of matches. "Tada!"

Roxy blinked and tried to think of something nice to say. "Um…"

"I thought you would be impressed," Zillo sounded genuinely hurt and Roxy stammered for a moment before she caught the gleam in his eye.

"Damn you Zillo!"

He laughed. "Sorry Roxy, I couldn't resist."

She did smack him then, though gently and in jest, on the arm, "well, what is it? Can you tell me how it works?"

"Gladly."

***

They returned to the main lobby, Roxy's head was filled with information and detailed instructions and many other things she didn't have the energy to deal with in the midst of everything else. She took note of the time on her wristlet and discovered she had spent much longer with Zillo than she had originally planned on.

Time flies when you're having fun, a voice whispered in her head. She told it to shut up.

"You should come back again... when this is all over, I mean. I'll give you the grand tour."

"I'd really like that," Roxy replied.

"No pressure eh, Roxy. Just a tour. That's it."

"I know Zillo." She knew he wanted more but he would never push.

"Best of luck, sweetheart. I hope it all works out for you. *All* of it." He raised a brow meaningfully.

Roxy knew that Zillo believed that there was unfinished business between her and Sam and perhaps he was right to a certain extent. "I've told you Zillo, that ship sailed long ago. It's gone so far that it's not even a speck out on the horizon." Roxy smiled sadly, but her voice held an air of finality and there was a flash of steely resolve in her eyes. She was slowly learning that she had to leave the past in the past. Once and for all. Where it belonged.

"Call me. Let me know how things go. And that you're okay."

"I will. I promise," Roxy replied, breathlessly. She turned to leave. Clinging to the package she'd acquired in the Daedalus Lab as if her very life depended on it. It probably did. Hers and Sam's and River's.

She didn't need to look back to know that Zillo was watching her leave. She knew he would watch through the window until she was long gone. She also knew that he wished she would stay.

The best she could offer was that she would come back ... in time.

The stomp of her boots against the concrete echoed down the street behind her and for a moment she faltered, squinting in the bright mid-day light of Suntwin. *Was this the right decision?* She asked herself for the millionth time. She swallowed hard against the lump in her throat. She was leaving behind what could very well be her future... to dive headlong into the churning, murky waters of her past.

This would be the last time.

Squaring her shoulders, she picked up the pace, and kept on walking.

CHAPTER SEVENTEEN

A siren blared. Someone nearby was playing music – very loudly. A succession of *SkyShaw's* zoomed by, their passengers whopping and laughing.

She didn't hear the approach from behind.

"You seem troubled, Ms. Buckles."

"That's a bit of an understatement." Roxy forcefully blew a breath out through her lips and ran a hand through her hair. She winced as a finger brushed against her still fresh head wound.

Roxy was reclining on the balcony of her condo; her feet propped up on the railing. River Lynx stepped through the sliding door and closed it behind them softly before padding to the railing and leaning against it. The night was balmy; the temperamental breeze was just enough to keep them from overheating. A glass of water next to Roxy was sitting in a pool of condensation, too tepid to drink now; she hadn't really wanted it anyways. She had poured it for something to do with her hands.

"Would you like to talk about it? I have been told that I am a good listener. It is okay to be vulnerable you know. It is not a sign of weakness."

Roxy shot River a covert look from beneath her lashes.

"Or I could contact a friend for you. If you would rather that. I think perhaps the time has come for you to unburden yourself of what is evidently weighing you down."

Roxy sighed in resignation. "No, no it's fine. I tried earlier but I can't get in touch with Suki at all. I've called the office, her house, and blipped her wristlet. Nothing. She's probably too busy working on the mess I left behind for her or maybe just too pissed off at me to talk. I'll give her some time to cool off." Roxy stood up and leaned against the railing, her shoulders tense. She was embarrassed to have admitted to River that she really only had one close friend.

Unless you counted Zillo.

Though Roxy wasn't sure exactly what he was to her at the moment. She knew what he *could* be – all she had to do was say the word. *But what about Sam?* Her traitorous heart whispered.

"Shut the fuck up," she muttered.

"What was that?" River inquired, as she glanced away from the view of New Cosmos. She had been intently studying a flock of biomorphic robotic birds that had just soared past.

"Sorry," Roxy blushed. "I was just talking to myself."

"It is very bright here on your planet," River observed. "And loud. On Mauw we cherish the silence. It is in the silence that we are able to hear what our heart and our mind have to say. We also very much enjoy naps. Sleep is restorative."

Roxy didn't know how to respond to that but she considered how New Cosmos might appear to outsiders. Roxy loved how *alive* Aurora was. How it never stopped moving, how it was never quiet, how it never slept.

She probably liked it for the very reasons that River did not.

Roxy looked at the earnest faced Mauwian standing across from her and did the exact opposite of what she would normally do: she spilled her guts. By the time she stopped her throat was raw and she felt a bone deep weariness that could only come from such a cathartic experience. She grabbed the glass of water and gulped it down.

"Ms. Buckles."

"River, after everything I just told you, I think it's fair to say you can call me Roxy now."

River nodded. "Roxy then. Your friend Suki is right to tell you to ask for help when you need it. You should listen to her. She sounds very smart. I also think that you yourself know that you cannot keep this up long term. It is not fair to Sam and it is not fair to your new friend Zebra."

"Zillo," Roxy interrupted.

"Yes, that's what I said," River nodded assuredly. "Neither is it fair to yourself, this situation you have come to find yourself in. Look, I know you are confused right now. A lot of information has come your way in a short period of time and you have every right to be distracted. But you cannot continue to string them along in this way."

Roxy dropped her head into her hands and groaned.

"And despite what you think, Roxy, *you* also deserve happiness." River remained silent for a moment, then gently asked, "Do you still love him? Sam, I mean."

Roxy pondered the question in tense silence and then, in clipped tones that belied the emotion beneath them, she finally replied, "I *made* myself hate him, you know. When I saw Suki, the way she was in her hospital bed. She looked so broken. We didn't even know if she was going to make it. And the way she struggled to learn how to do everything again - it really wasn't all that difficult to push him out of my heart." She cleared her throat against a sudden rush of tears. She would not cry. "A part of me will probably always love Sam, but its the part of me that I've had to lock away all these years. I'm afraid to open that door again."

"Sometimes the past needs to stay where it is," River nodded, gazing once again out over the vista of New Cosmos. "Now, Roxy, we really must do something about the state of your kitchen. You don't even have any…"

A call came through to Roxy's wristlet, startling them both. River went quiet as Roxy answered and replied to the caller in clipped tones.

"Trouble," they purred, more of a statement than a question, their whiskers twitching.

"Always is, River," Roxy replied, grimly. "Always is."

"What can I do to help?"

"Well, River, I'm going to need you to punch me in the face. Several times. Use the claws. And make it believable."

River's eyes grew wide with astonishment but then as realization set in, a toothy grin spread across their face. "It would be my pleasure."

CHAPTER EIGHTEEN

There was no hesitation in Roxy's stride as she stalked her way across the lobby of The Planetary Regulation Committee building. She did not pause beneath the large bulletin board screen this time, did not stop and gaze in awe at the opulence of the foyer or the rushing crowds inside the plaza. She did not acknowledge the shocked, open-mouthed expressions and audible gasps that resounded from the people as she passed.

She smashed a finger against the call button for the elevator and waited, the flare of her nostrils only a minor indication of the volcanic fury that bubbled just below the surface.

"Level 220," she barked when she had been permitted entry. The doors whooshed shut and Roxy stiffened her shoulders. *Deep breaths*, she muttered to herself. It was almost show time.

The elevator dinged, announcing her arrival, and she stepped into the lavish office for only the second time in her life. She feverishly hoped it would be the last.

"Roxy, you're returned already. Well done." Carmine emerged from his inner sanctum; Flavia was close on his heels. Flavia gave a muffled squeak as Carmine continued to speak, "I... uh... trust that you were successful in your endeavours?"

Roxy expected it was a rare occasion that found Commander Seth Carmine at a loss for words. She felt a rush of satisfaction. Roxy watched coolly as the Commander assessed her from head to toe. Roxy was covered in splatters of blood. As she moved, glimpses of raw looking scratches along her legs and arms could be seen inside the tatters of her clothing.

"It's done," Roxy confirmed.

A Cheshire grin spread slowly across Carmine's face and he rubbed his hands together in glee. Turning, he spoke in a low tone to Flavia who nodded and scurried out of the room. "Let's have a seat." He gestured towards the lounge area. "Uh... try not to get too much blood on the upholstery if you can help it."

Roxy plunked herself down on a white leather armchair, and leaned back pretending not to notice as Carmine's face blanched.

"Now, tell me, how did you do it – give me all the gory details. Did it beg for its life?" Carmine leaned forward, virtually salivating in anticipation.

Roxy had to suppress a shudder. "As you can probably tell from my appearance," Roxy gestured to her wounded arms and a trio of red scrapes that marred one cheek, "Lynx went down fighting." She forced a chuckle. Roxy began to describe, in painstak-

ing detail, the fabricated torture and eventual exter-
mination of River Lynx, a story they had constructed
together before they'd left Mauw. "So, then I grabbed
a fistful of fur and slit their throat."

Carmine leaned back against the sofa where he
sat, nodding appreciatively.

Roxy was appalled, both at the Commanders
unbridled delight at the description of such a cold-
blooded murder and also over her own ability to easily tell such bald-faced lies.

"I can see a very bright future for you with The
PRC Roxy. Very bright indeed." He rose from the
sofa and crossed to stand in front of the glass wall
that overlooked a stunning azure sky.

"Thank you, Commander." Roxy inclined her
head in acknowledgement. "There's just one more
thing though. Sam Sparrow. River Lynx has been harboring him on Mauw He has been conspiring with,
and aiding, The Bastent *this whole time*."

Roxy had to give it to Carmine, he had the grace
to at least try and look surprised by the revelation.
"That is incredible. And were you able to take care of
your little *problem* with him?"

"No. The bastard had already absconded from
Mauw by the time I'd beaten the info out of Lynx,"
Roxy growled, fists balled tightly in her lap. A dark
shadow passed over Carmine's face as Roxy dropped
the news; he quickly shuttered it, a stony mask taking its place. "I *was* able to ascertain exactly where he
has fled to Commander: Sam Sparrow is on *Aurora*.
And he's out for blood."

Carmine cleared his throat, a sheen of sweat glistened on his brow. "Is that so?"

"Yes," Roxy replied. "And from what I've heard, the blood that he's after… it's yours."

Time seemed to slow down. Roxy's heart beat a wild tattoo beneath her breast as she waited to see if Carmine would take the bait.

He laughed, but underneath the cool façade Roxy could detect a whiff of nervousness.

"Me?" Carmine questioned. "Why… why would Sparrow come after me?"

"He seems to be harboring some delusion that *you* are responsible for the explosion at The Academy." Roxy injected as much disbelief as she could manage into her speech. "He's claiming that *you* set *him* up."

"That's preposterous," Carmine spluttered, turning to gaze out the window. Roxy watched in amusement as he reached up to loosen his tie.

Hook, line and sinker, Roxy thought. "Of course. Imagine the audacity," she exclaimed. "As if anyone would believe some filthy criminal like him over you, a respectable businessman and leader."

"Thank you, Roxy for your – "

"One other thing though," Roxy interrupted, lips pursed in thought. "He's claiming to have proof of his innocence. Surveillance videos that had previously been doctored; witnesses who have since come forward to say that their testimony was a lie and that they'd been paid well to do so. It's quite damning."

Carmine swung around; eyes narrowed as he assessed Roxy. "Well obviously he's full of shit."

"Yes," Roxy remarked. "Something definitely stinks here."

Carmine tightened his tie, fiddled with the cufflinks at his wrist and rebuttoned his jacket. "He *must* be stopped."

"Well, lucky for you Commander, you already know someone who's perfect for the job." Roxy grinned, gathering her focus.

She saw Carmine visibly relax. "Indeed, I do."

Roxy stood. "I have some leads I plan to follow up on this evening. I'll be in touch."

"Please do Roxy. And thank you for cleaning up this mess. From the moment we met, I knew you wouldn't mind getting a little dirty," he winked. "You never let them get away, do you?"

"No, and you can count on that." Roxy threw over her shoulder as she strutted out of the room and through the doors of the waiting elevator, shoulders back and her head held high. "I *always* get my man."

CHAPTER NINETEEN

The pain behind her temples throbbed in time with the wailing of the alarm. Suki massaged her forehead and the bridge of her nose with little success at alleviating either the pain or the annoyance.

Reorganizing a schedule that had already been reorganized to within an inch of its life was pushing Suki's patience to its limits. She loved Roxy. She loved her job but... Suki leaned back in her chair with a sigh and for a moment allowed herself to fantasize about what life might have been like. What would have happened if she'd been able to graduate from The Academy. Where would she be right now if things had gone according to plan?

She'd applied to The Academy on a whim. Their training programs were second to none and her friends had already been accepted. Her marks were good enough for a scholarship and so she'd written the entrance exam. How far would she have gone – would she have risen to the top? Would she now be teaching at The Academy if Sam Sparrow hadn't blown it to smithereens? Truth of the matter was, after so long – it didn't really matter anymore. She may not have gone where she intended but right now, she was exactly where she needed to be.

Suki tapped on the buttons on her intercom with more force than necessary and waited not so patiently for a response at the other end.

"We are sorry Ms. Kwan. We're still working on it."

"It's been an hour."

"Again, I am sorry. I have everyone in security working on it. We can't figure out why the alarm is going off. We may need for push a full restart of the system."

"How long?" Suki demanded.

He sighed. "I can't say for sure. Look, most places have closed up shop for the day. Maybe you might consider doing the same?"

"Not a chance," Suki muttered before she ended the call, her gaze taking in the myriad of papers strewn across her desk, the two glowing screens showing the color-coded schedule she still had to completely reorganize. She'd be lucky to get home for bedtime.

The wail for the alarm continued through the afternoon. Suki typed and filed at a breakneck speed, not even pausing for lunch. As Suntwin finally set over the bustling downtown metropolis, Suki leaned back in her chair and sighed in relief. Her work for the day was done.

She quickly turned off her screens and carefully arranged her paperwork into three neat piles: *Urgent, slightly less urgent,* and *can wait.* She was contemplating dinner when it happened.

If not for the growling of her stomach, Suki might have thought she'd gone deaf in the ensuing silence. The cessation of the alarm was a welcome relief. It would have been even more welcome – Suki glanced at her wristlet – seven hours ago.

The pounding pressure that had wrapped itself around Suki's forehead like a band had only increased as the day wore on. She thought longingly of stuffing her face with something sinful and collapsing atop her bed with the relief of a *No-Graine* strip stuck to her forehead. It would knock her out until morning; a welcome reprieve.

Suki had already tapped in the first three digits of the alarm code before she noticed it was not illuminated as usual. The eerie green light was absent in the dimness of the office as Suki lowered the overheads with the wave of her hand.

Security had obviously opted for a restart of the system. Suki carefully treaded her way back to the desk and pulled a set of tarnished keys from within a deep drawer. They were fossils in Suki's opinion, archaic and unnecessary, left over from a bygone era but Roxy insisted on keeping them in case of an emergency. Suki would never be able to tell her about this – she'd never live it down.

It took her a few minutes to figure out the mechanics. She found the correct key for the office door and smiled, pleased, as the rarely used lock slid into place with a satisfying clunk.

"How quaint." Suki tossed the ring of keys into her satchel and exited the building, thinking that the alarm system would be back up and running in the morning, the keys could be returned to the place at the back of the drawer and Roxy would never have to know she'd been right about them.

And if Marcus told her, well... Suki smirked. Yeah, that wouldn't happen on her watch.

***

The murky grey dawn that greeted Suki the following morning did nothing to stifle her cheery mood. It had just turned 5 am, her headache was gone and thinking ahead to her day, Suki knew she had only three items on her desk marked as urgent. Maybe she'd grab lunch on the Esplanade this afternoon. An extra-long lunch to make up for yesterday. She'd charge it to Roxy's business account. Satisfied with her plan, Suki quickly dressed, slicked a sheen of lipstick across her lips, pulled her dark hair into a sleek chignon and decided she felt well enough today to leave for work with just her cane.

She arrived at the office, looking forward to the day ahead, for once. When her ID card failed to allow her entry, she shielded her eyes, trying to peer into the exterior beyond the glare of the reflective glass. No one in sight. She banged on the main door and when this yielded no results, she used her wristlet to call the main operator. The disembodied voice of the automated answering system informed her in a monotone voice that there was currently no one available to take her call.

The electronic buzz that accompanied the opening of the main door finally reached her ears.

"About bloody time," she muttered, trying to see into the interior to thank the good Samaritan who'd let her in.

"Marcus!"

"Sorry Ms. Kwan. Still having some issues. The whole building is operating on backup. At least the alarm stopped sounding?" His attempt at a joke failing, the grin on his face dissolved in the shadow of Suki's displeasure.

"Please excuse me Marcus, I have work to do."

Fishing the ancient set of keys from her satchel, Suki let herself into the office, flicking on the overhead lights. She strolled to the desk, powering up her screens. She noted a surprising lack of messages requiring her attention and nodded her head in approval.

Suki sniffed. Something smelled repulsive. Had she inadvertently missed a glob of LanQuid goo when she'd cleaned up? No. That wasn't it. It was more like spoiled food masked by some off brand air freshener or body odor mixed with cheap cologne. Suki froze. A frisson of fear tingled along her spine.

A shadow moved behind the shades in Roxy's office.

Suki was not alone.

She reached for the alarm button beneath her desk only to realize, her stomach sinking, that it would be of no use with the entire security system down. Suki muttered a curse beneath her breath and began backing up towards the door.

"I don't think that's a very good idea, Ms. Kwan."

Suki whipped around, "Marcus!"

He had the grace to look embarrassed. "I needed the money. My daughter. She wants to go to school on Earth." He shrugged. "That shit ain't cheap."

Suki heard the door to Roxy's office swing open and a large greasy Cro-Magnon type grinned at her, cracking his knuckles. With alarm, Suki realized the man was wearing the uniform of the PRC Gendarme. Her heartrate spiked. He wasn't even attempting to hide his identity. Which meant her didn't care that Suki knew who he was.

That wasn't a good sign.

She tried to stall, distract them, hoping they wouldn't notice her activate the emergency alert on her wristlet.

"That door was locked!"

Marcus and the Gendarme chuckled together companionably. "Those old locks are easy to breech."

The Gendarme rushed forward and wrenched her arm behind her back. He had moved so fast for a beast of his size that Suki barely had time to register the sharp pain in her shoulder before he had relieved her of her wristlet and tossed it to Marcus.

Suki's cane clattered to the floor.

"You said she keeps a chair here?" the Gendarme growled.

"Yes." Marcus fumbled with the closet door, producing a compact wheelchair Suki used on particularly bad days. "See JB! Told you!"

The Gendarme grunted in satisfaction. "Put her in it. We've got places to be." He sneered at Suki and licked his lips.

There'd be no long relaxing lunch for Suki on the Esplanade today.

If ever.

CHAPTER TWENTY

What the hell? Roxy thought as she stood outside the entrance to her condo. She was sure she'd heard yelling inside and then, *was that a hiss?*

The atmosphere inside Roxy's condo was thick with tension when she walked in. She could have cut it with a *karambit*. She found Sam pacing the room like a caged animal while River was doing their best to get him to sit down, to eat something, drink some water; anything other than this frenetic marching from one end of the room to the other.

River had not been impressed to find a half-empty fridge with nothing more than a few languishing bunches of kale, expired condiments, beer and crusty take-out food, still in its containers. They'd been forced to settle for an old can of tuna, found languishing at the back of a cupboard, probably expired. It still sat, uneaten, on the table in front of them.

Sam rushed to Roxy's side as she walked in the door, his expression hesitant but hopeful. "Well?"

"He bought it." Just saying the words out loud to someone instead of merely thinking them gave her a rush of energy and excitement. It was the best part of the job.

She glanced at her wristlet. "My contacts are now on site. We'll give it a little bit of time to do their normal thing and then one of them will rush to report that you've been sighted at the old grounds of The Academy. Carmine won't want to do the dirty work himself, I'm sure; he's too much of a coward. He'll leave that up to me, that's why he wanted me in on this to begin with - but I don't think he'll be able to resist turning up to confront you and lord it over you that he's 'won'."

"And then it will all be over," Sam whispered, wonder in his voice. "Finally."

Roxy met River's eyes across the room and an unspoken promise passed between them. Tonight, they would make things right... one way or another.

***

The cool air was stark relief against her flushed cheeks. It had been a long but fruitful day. Roxy stood on the balcony gazing out over the blinding lights of New Cosmos, the faint sounds of late-night revellers rising up to greet her. She smiled. The city never stopped. She couldn't think of anywhere else that she would rather live.

"Roxy..."

She froze, her name so raw upon Sam's lips that it sent her stomach into a somersault.

"We should talk."

This again; he was relentless. Roxy braced herself

because he wasn't going to be happy with what she had to say. "I didn't realize you enjoyed my conversation quite so much, Sparrow."

"Cut it out Roxy. I know what you're doing. You only call me *Sparrow* when you're trying to shut me out. I know you've had a lot thrown at you over the past few days. You haven't had as much time as I've had to process this whole mess."

"I am fine."

"Are you really though Roxy? Because I see your hands shake when you brush back your hair or when you lift a glass or pick up a file. I see that faraway look you get in your eye when you think no one is looking because you've gone some place inside your own head." Sam sighed, his frustration mounting. "Come on. Talk to me."

"I am so tired, Sam. Tired of talking, tired of being in the dark and being the last to know everything. I *need* to finish this. Once it's all over, then there will be time to talk."

"Why do you have to be so goddamned stubborn, Roxy?" Sam slammed a hand against the railing, his shoulders tense and his face grim. "What about us then?"

"Us?" Roxy laughed, though she found little humor in the situation. She turned her back to gaze out at the cityscape, the lights and the buildings filled with people. She wondered what they were all doing tonight. If they were happy. Truly happy. Or just living a lie like she had been for so long. "There is no *us* Sam. Not anymore."

"Are you sure about that?" he whispered, his voice low and husky.

"Yes," she replied, firmly, wanting to shut this down before it even got started. But the quaver in her voice betrayed her.

"Is there someone else? Is that why?" Sam asked. He held his breath waiting for a sign from Roxy that his worst nightmare hadn't come true. That he had lost her once and for all, that the one last thread of hope that he had been holding on to had been permanently severed.

The silence grew. And with it, Sam's confidence that Roxy still felt *something* for him.

Roxy felt Sam draw nearer, step up closer behind her; it was a subtle movement but, then again, she had always been in tune with the movements of his body.

"You should get some rest Sam. You'll need it. I have things to do."

"Do you really? What things to do you need to do?"

"There's a lot that needs to be done tonight," she insisted.

"Do you *want* to go Roxy?" Sam asked.

Roxy turned around, her eyes pleading: "Don't do this Sam, please. It's not the time."

"Do what?" He stepped closer, and then closer still, until they were barely a hair's breadth apart. "This?"

Sam ran one calloused finger down Roxy's jawline, stroked it gently across her bottom lip. Her breath caught in her throat.

"Or this?"

He leaned towards her until his forehead touched hers. She closed her eyes, memories rushing back. Happier times. Her and Sam.

"Or this?"

His lips brushed against hers tentatively, seeking her permission. She sighed and leaned into the kiss, deepening it. She felt a shudder pass through him and thrilled at the knowledge that she could still make him feel this way. She felt powerful and alive. She slid her hands up his broad chest and across his shoulders before reaching up to tangle her fingers in his hair; she tugged gently on the too long locks, scraping her nails across his scalp; he groaned and nipped at her bottom lip. He spread his hands across her back, and then lower still, crushing her against him.

Sam trailed a line of scorching kisses from the corner of her mouth, and along her neck pausing to taste the pulse raging above her collarbone. He broke the connection, his breathing ragged, "stay with me tonight?" he pleaded. "I've missed you."

Roxy met his eyes, heavy-lidded with desire. This loaded question; she knew it was about far more than just tonight. And she didn't have an answer. Especially not the answer she knew he wanted. She dragged her tangled hair out of her face, took a deep breath and moved from Sam's embrace, stepping towards to the door that led back inside.

"I can't do this Sam. I'm sorry."

She closed her eyes before she could see the expression on his face. She hated seeing him in so much pain. She stepped back through the door and left him there, alone, on the balcony.

And though she wanted to, she did not look back.

CHAPTER TWENTY-ONE

Suki swam to consciousness slowly, like a deep-sea diver ascending from the briny depths. Her head felt impossibly heavy; her ears stuffed full of cotton, her mouth dry and her tongue like sandpaper. She'd kill for a blob of *Quencher* right about now. Or two. The feeling was quite similar to the worst hangover she had ever experienced... only Suki didn't drink anymore, and she hadn't taken a sip of alcohol in well over ten years. Her eyes popped open as reality slammed into her.

She vaguely recalled the pinprick of a needle and reached up to rub her neck. There was a tender spot - an injection site - a few inches below her left ear.

She'd been drugged.

Recalling the scene back at the office, ambushed by the head of security and that disgusting piece of garbage, JB, Suki used her anger to bolster some courage. She put her hands to the floor and pushed herself into a sitting position. A gasp escaped her lips; the flare of pain in her hip was fresh and sharp – she gritted her teeth and kept pushing. Leaning back against the wall, sweat beading on her forehead, she breathed a sigh of relief, thankful for small blessings.

If she somehow managed to get out of this alive, she was going to make sure that Marcus got his ass fired. And then sent off to Brig-5 as fast as humanly possible. Scum like that deserved to rot in prison.

"Suki shivered. The room was pitch black and the tantalizing sound of dripping water resounded somewhere close-by. She licked her chapped lips. She was desperate enough to consider it. A foul stench of oil and rubber permeated the air and Suki tried to breath though her mouth. She was beginning to realize the enormity of the situation that she was in, but Suki simply did not have it in her to give up easily.

She raised her hands, waved them around slowly, reaching blindly out in front of her. She scooted herself forward a few inches, ignoring the pain, and repeated the action. If there was chair, a table, or some other piece of furniture she might be able to use it to haul herself up. After lying prone on a cold stone floor for an extended period of time, her muscles had seized up, her legs less than cooperative, failing to follow her commands to *move*. What she would do once she had managed to accomplish that feat? *Well,* Suki thought, *we shall cross that bridge when we come to it.*

The echo of approaching footsteps snagged her attention and, knowing she had mere moments, she slid herself backwards and eased her body back onto the floor, to make herself look as pathetic and defenseless as possible. She heard an old manual lock disengaging, the click of a switch, and then light flooded the room, blinding her. She raised a hand to shield her eyes against the sudden glare.

"Rise and shine, sleeping beauty."

Suki recognized the guttural tones of the apostate Gendarme who, in cahoots with Marcus, had kidnapped her and taken her... wherever she was right now. She blinked up at him and then surreptitiously looked around the room. It was completely bare, the floor filthy and covered in debris, a leak in the far corner moldered its way down the wall. Suki was glad she hadn't gotten that far.

And she was certainly thankful that she happened to be up to date on all her vaccinations.

"Get up."

"I can't get up, you stupid prick," Suki spat, bristling at being ordered to do anything for this barbarian. "In case you haven't noticed...?" She gestured wildly to her legs, crumpled beneath her.

"You're spunky. I like you."

Roxy rolled her eyes. "The feeling is *not* mutual."

He had no weapon that she could see but she was harboring no allusion that she would be able to take down this behemoth of a man all on her own. She would just have to bide her time until the moment came, when the feeling came back to her feet and her hands weren't so still. She would know when. *They hadn't killed you yet*, she surmised, *so obviously I am meant to serve some other purpose*. She would try and use that to her advantage.

He lurched toward her and Suki willed herself not

to cower beneath his towering frame. She would not give him the satisfaction of knowing just how scared she was. He grabbed her by the arm.

A small cry of pain escaped her. "Watch it asshole."

He hauled her up from the floor as though she weighed nothing.

"I suppose Marcus is back at The Chaffey Building now, working as if nothing ever happened?" she asked, trying to stall for time. "There never was a problem with the security system, was there?"

"Can't get nothing past you, hey?" JB smirked and jerked her forward, wrenching her shoulder. "But I'm afraid our friend Marcus has outlived his usefulness. He's had a bit of an *unfortunate accident* earlier this afternoon. Now shut the hell up and start walking."

Suki limped from the room, pain shooting from hips to ankles, pins and needles in her calves; her left foot still partially numb. JB half supported, half dragged her from the room before unceremoniously dumping her into the wheelchair he'd stolen from the office.

He pulled a rag from his back pocket. "As much as I have enjoyed our chat little lady, I'm going to need you to be extra quiet now, got it?" He stuffed the rag in her mouth, walked around to the back of the chair and pushed her toward what looked like a large service elevator.

Suki tried not to gag as the cloth pressed against the back of her throat. She blinked the water out of her eyes and as they adjusted to the dim light of this new location, she tried not to let on that she knew exactly where they were.

The storage units on the lower levels of The PRC Plaza.

Realization slammed into Suki with the force of a battering ram.

This was an inside job.

Roxy was gonna be pissed.

CHAPTER TWENTY-TWO

"Would you like a caf-tab or a regular coffee?" Roxy offered, shifting from one foot to another in the middle of the kitchen.

She was in no mood to play hostess but anything to break the damnable silence that had hung like a heavy cloud over her condo since she'd returned from her first visit to CommsLink.

Sam leaned his elbows on the table, ran a hand over his face. He looked exhausted. "No Roxy, I don't want coffee. I want to…"

A sharp beep emitted from Roxy's wristlet and she quickly pressed a button to silence it.

Saved by the bell.

Her face hardened as she read the message that had arrived with the notification. She glanced up and her eyes locked on Sparrow's. He had a way of looking at her that was equal parts want and what the hell. It was not something Roxy was ready to deal with quite yet, especially after what had happened earlier in the night. And especially after her stolen moments with Zillo. There was enough on her plate already.

She quickly looked away, calling out to River Lynx who was napping in the other room: "Lynx! It's time."

The trap had been set. It was now or never. Sam and River grabbed their bags and with a nod at Roxy to indicate that they were ready, followed her out of the condo. They would bypass the front doors of the building – too risky – and instead a *Roamer* (an off duty rapid transit *SkyShaw* driver looking to make a little extra cash) would collect them from the roof and deliver them across the city, no questions asked.

Thunder rumbled in the distance and a streak of lightening kissed the sky in brilliant hues of violet and blue. River eyed the swirling mass of murky pregnant clouds above their heads with concern. Under different circumstances Roxy might have been amused. Clearly, the idea of a rain storm did not appeal to Lynx. Roxy was really starting to like that feline.

"We'll test the device when we arrive." Roxy, sitting between River and Sam, spoke low so the *Roamer* wouldn't overhear.

Sam gave a curt nod. Roxy wondered for a moment if he might be nervous but then dismissed it just as quickly. He'd never been the type.

The plan was simple: Roxy and River would secret themselves amongst the ruins of The Academy, staying within earshot should Sam need assistance. Sam's job was to allow Carmine to "catch" him hiding there. Carmine would use it as an opportunity to gloat of course, to lord it over Sam that he, Carmine, had finally won. They just needed him to say the words and the entire confession would be broadcast live across every single electronic device on Aurora via the CommsLink System wired to Sam. Roxy had called in a *big* favor.

Carmine was going down.

"We got this." She said aloud, to assure herself as much as the two sitting beside her. She felt Sam grab her hand and squeeze.

This time, she couldn't bring herself to pull away.

***

The *Roamer* set them down half a mile from the former grounds of The Academy. The driver grinned at the generous tip and zipped away whistling a jaunty tune, the extra money ensuring his discretion.

Sam was a bag of nerves. He paced and ran his hands over his head as Roxy and River discussed the whens and wheres of their mission using the projected map on Roxy's wristlet.

In the moments before they walked down to the road, their final steps before the denouement of this wretched night, River pulled Sam gently to one side, paw on his shoulder as they spoke in hushed tones. Roxy saw Sam nod and the two embraced. She tamped down on the wave of jealously that threatened to swamp her. *You forfeited that particular right, Buckles*, she admonished herself. She quickly turned away.

"Let's test that CommsLink System shall we?"

Roxy called over her shoulder.

Sam approached, hauling his shirt over his head.

Roxy cleared her throat. "So, uh, this small patch gets applied to the chest right... uh... here and is absorbed by the skin. It remains an active mic for three hours." She pressed the thin membrane against Sam's chest. His skin was warm and alive beneath her fingers. She snatched her hand back as though she'd been burned.

She heard Sam chuckle as he put his shirt back on.

"Don't you start." Roxy snapped.

"How'd you swing this anyways?" Sam asked. "This kind of equipment is above even your pay grade."

"I know a guy," Roxy said with finality. And boy did she owe Zillo big time.

"A guy hey? What kind of guy?"

Roxy's eyes flashed. "A friend. Not that it's any of your business."

"It *is* my business if you've dragged some stranger into this whole thing without... "

"I would never," Roxy snapped. "He owns CommsLink and he wanted to help. He's a good guy. Not that you'd know anything about that."

"Hey, now that's not fair Roxy." Sam sounded genuinely affronted.

"Okay lovebirds." River interjected, rolling their eyes. "Are we ready to go now?"

Roxy glared at them but bit back her retort. "As much as we will ever be," she finally replied, her mouth set in a grim line.

Sam hefted a backpack onto his shoulder. "This is going to work… right?"

Neither of them replied. The time for reassurances had long passed.

They set off at a steady pace, one in front of the other with Roxy taking the lead. They kept to the shelter of the treeline, at the side of the road. There were fissures in the asphalt, weeds snaking through the cracks; the trees at the sides, once trimmed and neat, now lorded in a canopy over the road. As they passed through the broken and twisted gates, the hulk of the former Academy slowly emerged from the darkness.

The smell of ash and smoke and death still hung heady on the air. Or perhaps it was just an olfactory memory for Roxy, throwing her back in time as the sights and sounds of that terrible day all came back to her in a flash:

"My friends! You have to help them!"

"Were they down here with you?" The man in the high-tech rescue gear had to yell to be heard above the whir of rescue helicopters over head and the sirens of emergency vehicles on the ground.

"No… no they were on the 180th floor."

The look on his face told her all that she needed to know.

"No. You need to do something. Now." Roxy coughed, the deep hacking by-product of smoke inhalation. Blood poured from a gash at her hairline, dripped into her eyes; bloody tears ran down her cheeks, cutting tracks through

the mask of dust and soot that covered her face.

"Ma'am, you should really be seen by the medi-droid."

"Well, sir, you should really suck my – "

The blast shook the ground beneath their feet, nearly knocked them to the ground.

"Secondary device. I repeat, a second bomb. Fall back, fall back!" The guy screamed into his comms, turned and waved his arms for the rest of his men to follow as they headed for cover.

And Roxy, well, Roxy turned and ran back into the building.

Or what was left of it anyways.

"Wow." Sam's soft shocked exhalation right next to her ear snapped Roxy back to reality with a jolt.

She had almost forgotten the enormity of the destruction the explosion had caused. She was glad she wasn't seeing it in the harsh reality of daylight. A shudder passed through her as she took a deep breath, seeking equilibrium.

The past and the present were colliding and Roxy was holding on for dear life, trying to ground herself in the here and now.

"Places everyone," Roxy muttered, low and deliberate. "Let's do this."

The scrape of a boot behind them, then, "Fancy meeting you here, Roxy Buckles."

Well fuck.

CHAPTER TWENTY-THREE

Commander Seth Carmine materialized from behind a towering pile of scorched rubble like a magician emerging from a cloud of smoke; smarmy and with a cocksure swagger – the only thing missing was the cape and top hat. He snapped his fingers and his tall, lumbering assistant emerged from the overgrown foliage across the blackened courtyard. The flunky had greasy dark hair, It was slicked back from a sloping forehead; his burly muscles rippled beneath the garish green uniform of The PRC Gendarme that he was wearing and a twisted smile spread across his face.

In front of him, weeping softly behind a gag stuffed in her mouth was Suki Kwan.

"Suki!" Roxy took a step forward, her intentions quite clear, but stopped short at the sight of the large, wickedly sharp knife that the Gendarme had pulled from behind his back. She realized, to her chagrin, that Seth Carmine had also devised a plan. And it looked like his was the only one going accordingly. Roxy would never forgive herself if her own hubris got Suki killed.

"Now, now Roxy." Carmine tsk-tsked. "Behave yourself. If you keep that up, JB there might have to use that knife. And trust me, you do not want JB to use his knife. Are we clear?"

"Very." The word was spat through clenched teeth as Roxy tried to stave off the combination of intense anger and fear pooling in her stomach.

"Please remove the weapon you have holstered on your thigh and slide it towards me."

Roxy stared at him; her chin tipped in defiance.

JB brandished the knife towards Suki with gleeful exuberance. Roxy felt River Lynx slide closer to her and whisper, "You may not want to *chaton*, but you must do as he says."

With a deep sigh Roxy acquiesced. She unclipped her weapon and flung it as far as she could behind her. There was no way in hell she was giving Carmine and his goon any extra ammunition.

"Not very good at following orders, are you?" Carmine asked, incensed.

Roxy quirked an eyebrow and shrugged.

"You want your friend over there to die right now?" He nodded towards Suki. "All I have to do is say the word."

Sam let loose with a string of curses but was instantly drowned out by a sharp crack of thunder. The ground trembled beneath their feet and Roxy's nose detected a faint whiff of ozone.

An opportune distraction that River Lynx seemed more than happy to take advantage of: while the sky still grumbled and while gazes were drawn towards the dusky blue, River touched Roxy on the shoulder reassuringly and then bounded off into the shadows, disappearing out of sight; the tip of their tail blending in quickly amongst the tall willowy grass.

Perfect, Roxy thought to herself, *at least something is going according to plan... even if everything else has gone to shit.*

"You really seem to draw these cowardly types to you, don't you Roxy?" Carmine sniggered, his expression one of distaste. "Perhaps it would be wise of you to find yourself some better friends." The Gendarme joined in on the joke, cackling, though Roxy was certain, being more brawn than brains, that he knew absolutely nothing about that was actually going on.

"You applying for the job, Commander?" Roxy snarked. "Sorry, but your resume leaves a little something to be desired."

Shooting daggers in Roxy's direction, his face flushed an ungodly shade of purple, Carmine pulled himself to his full height: "You should be so lucky to be a part of my inner circle."

Roxy laughed. "Stuck a nerve, did I? You see, it doesn't count when you *pay* people for their loyalty, Commander. You really think JB over there would have your back if you didn't have him on the payroll?"

Carmine stammered. Roxy saw his eyes shift to JB and narrow.

JB, slack-jawed with incomprehension, did not

exactly inspire confidence.

A shout: Suki had somehow managed to free a hand from her bindings, yanking the gag from her mouth. "Look out!"

Roxy barely had time to register the movement before Sam exploded past her, knocking her to one side. She stumbled, blinked, and before she had a chance to process what was happened, Sam had launched himself at Carmine, slamming into him at full speed – the small handgun that Carmine had pulled from inside his coat tumbled away into the rubble.

Both men tumbled to the ground in a tornado of fists and fury.

Roxy heard Suki's frantic exclamations as she worked to free herself from her second binding. Sam had pinned Carmine beneath him. Grasping one of the Commanders lapels in a tight grip, he used his other fist to smash repeatedly into Carmine's face. A jagged flash of lightening zig-zagged across the sky, illuminating the scene in sporadic bursts, momentarily blinding Roxy.

She watched the chaos with mounting terror.

The gargantuan Gendarme backhanded Suki, her chair rocking back on its wheels from the force of the blow. She cupped her face, her right eye already beginning to swell. JB didn't spare her a backwards glance as he ran to his boss' aid.

Wincing in pain, Suki determinedly returned to working on the tape that still held her left wrist. Roxy surged forward, sprinting across the distance that separated them. She bent down and began wrenching at the tape.

"Roxy. Roxy, you have to help Sam. I can finish this. Please!"

"I've almost got it," Roxy insisted, as she felt the tape start to rip.

"Go, dammit. I've got this."

Roxy cursed, turning towards the scene that was playing out across the courtyard. She could do nothing but stand there as JB flung Carmine to safety behind him and suddenly surged forward, slamming his knife into Sam's back in one smooth brutal motion.

Roxy heard someone scream.

In an instant, she realized that the bloodcurdling cry had come from her.

Sam bucked as the knife sliced through his skin, the soft area just between his shoulder blades. He twisted away from Carmine, who lay heaving on the ground, spitting out blood and what might have been teeth. JB leaned over and yanked the knife out of Sam's back. Sam rolled over and away from Carmine; fists already clenched – ready for another fight.

Only he didn't get the chance.

JB dropped to the ground and straddled Sam, smashing the hilt of the weapon into his face. The Gendarme's greasy hair hung in his face; his eyes gleamed as he held the knife aloft.

Carmine pulled himself to his feet, swiped his sleeve across his lips and grinned through a mouth of bloodied teeth. He threw back his head and laughed maniacally.

A madman.

"Finish it." Carmine gave the order with relish.

"With pleasure boss."

"No!" The ragged howl burst from Roxy's throat as the Gendarme plunged the knife into Sam for the second time. Sam coughed, choking, as a mist of blood plumed from his mouth, splattering over his chin.

The ruthless assault had taken only seconds.

Roxy heard Sam call out her name.

But she had already started to move.

CHAPTER TWENTY-FOUR

Thunder detonated above them; lightning clawed its way across the dusk in jagged bursts as night claimed its dominance over the sky.

Roxy let loose with a primal battle cry as she ran and leaped onto JB's back, her arms encircling his trunk-like neck as he struggled to his feet, her weight throwing him off balance. Out of the corner of her eye she saw Carmine scrambling, searching frantically amongst the rubble for the small pistol he'd lost earlier.

JB jerked around, trying to shake her loose. He tossed his head, attempted to grab at her with his beefy hands; his broad shoulders and chest leaving him at a disadvantage. He was also dumb as fuck and evidently not used to people fighting back. Roxy dug her knees into his sides and held on for dear life. She clawed at his face with her nails and bit into his ear, gnawing viciously; gone half feral with grief and anger and fear.

The Gendarme roared. Roxy spat blood and gristle to the ground and screamed for River. "Lynx!

Now would be a good time to show yourself, god damn it."

Carmine sauntered over to Sam, who had rolled and was now trying to drag himself towards the madness. Roxy had no idea how he was still moving.

"I win, Sparrow." Carmine drew back his boot and smashed it into Sam's ribs with a sickening crack. He straightened his tie, smoothed down the front of his jacket, seemingly oblivious to the bloodstains that marred it.

JB abruptly stopped trying to toss Roxy from his back. He went still, as though making a decision, then threw himself backwards. Roxy had no time to react. She hit the ground with a sickening thud, the air rushing from her lungs as the hulking mass of the Gendarme landed on top of her. Instinctively she let go, gasping for breath. JB rolled to his knees and bent over Roxy, sneering at her as blood dripped from his ear. "Fucking cunt."

Roxy saw the fist coming towards her in slow motion. Pain ricocheted through her jaw as the punch landed with devastating accuracy. Her teeth snapped against her tongue and blood flooded her mouth. She closed her eyes against the wave of pain.

"Nice work JB! Carmine nodded at his cohort in approval. "Now take care of that other bitch."

Suki, who was tugging frantically at the last vestiges of tape that held her to the chair, flinched as the Gendarme sent a wolfish grin in her direction. "Happy to. Been waitin' all day."

And that was when the heavens opened up.

A stormy gust of wind surged over them, rain hammered against Roxy as she lay on the ground, plastering her hair to her scalp. She gasped as the icy water drenched her, thankful though she was for the clarity it brought. She clambered to her knees.

Sam was on the ground a short distance away, silent and still as a pool of blood expanded beneath him. He'd gone down fighting, the way he would have wanted. The knowledge did not make Roxy feel any better. She wanted to run to him, curl up by his side and tell him that everything would be okay. Old habits died hard. She forced herself to push him from her mind.

She locked eyes with Suki across the battered ruins of the once magnificent Academy for Intergalactic Law Enforcement. JB stood behind her, his knuckles fisted in her dark tresses; he had nearly lifted her out of her chair as he pressed the tip of his knife into the delicate skin at the base of her throat, just waiting for the word to cut.

"Look what happens when you double cross *me*." Carmine sneered as he towered over Roxy. "All you had to do was follow my instructions. You could have gone places. Now the only place you're going is the morgue."

"Tell him to let her go." Roxy's voice oozed malice. "She's done nothing to you."

"I'm afraid I can't do that Roxy," Carmine replied, amused. "She's my insurance policy, you see. And now, she knows just a little bit too much."

Where the hell was River? Roxy squinted into the

driving rain, straining to see beyond the shadows of the charred brick walls, rising jagged from the broken foundation. A dark sleek shape appeared suddenly before merging fluidly back under the cover of darkness. Roxy wondered if she had hallucinated it. Or maybe, just maybe, help *was* coming after all.

She needed to stall.

"Why?" Roxy staggered to her feet. "You owe us that much don't you think?" She didn't dare look back at Suki. Perhaps, if Roxy could hold Carmine's attention for long enough, she could buy some time for her.

This was all her fault.

She'd been arrogant.

And now her friends would pay the price. Guilt enveloped her.

Focus, Roxy, Focus, she admonished herself.

"I don't owe you a damned thing, Buckles but the answer to the question should be obvious, especially to you. You're all about *justice*," he mocked, rolling his eyes. "The *Academy*. What a joke. Churning out brainless twats who memorized and then regurgitated the very laws they had no intention of upholding; a mockery of the uniform they had the privilege of wearing. It had to stop."

Roxy blinked the rain from her eyes and stared at him, baffled. She was drenched to the skin. Under the umbrella of his own audacity, Carmine seemed unaffected by the downpour.

"Wait. You're telling me, you *broke* the law because you wanted to *uphold* the law?" She asked, incredulous. "But that's preposterous. People died! *Good* people. And not only that – you destroyed a man's life. A *good* man." Roxy didn't dare glance at the motionless form of Sam Sparrow sprawled out on the ground. She swallowed, hard. "There had to have been an easier way than that."

"Collateral damage." He shrugged, indifferent. "It was for the greater good. There was no need for a training academy. A waste of time and money. I could have easily handpicked our law enforcement to ensure we had the cream of the crop. Like I do now. It works well."

"Works well for *you*, I'm sure, but what about everyone else?" Roxy retorted, swiping rain from her eyes. "How many others have you double crossed or set up... or murdered to get your own way?"

"I'm right and you know it." He argued, ignoring her accusations. "Do you really think scum like Sam Sparrow, the so called *best* that The Academy had to offer, would have brought anything other than shame and embarrassment to The PRC? Strutting around like a cock of the walk. Useless piece of shit. What's a few casualties when you end up winning the war. Give up this ridiculous fight. I might even reconsider bringing you into the fold... if you're willing to follow my rules." Carmine raised an eyebrow, a self-satisfied smirk playing across his bloodied lips.

"No fucking way," Roxy spat, enunciating each word.

"Then I guess *you'll* get what's coming to *you*."

"No, Commander, you'll get what's coming to

you." Roxy gloated, as River Lynx glided from the shadows behind Carmine, stealthy and silent. They pounced; claws extended. Seizing him around the neck in a lethal grip, Lynx dragged him backwards and off balance. They hissed into Carmine's ear, whispering sweet nothings – but there would be nothing sweet about the plans they had for him.

Roxy saw his eyes go wide.

Gotcha.

CHAPTER TWENTY-FIVE

The deluge ended just as suddenly as it had begun: a tempest in a teapot. In the ensuing silence, the echo of a gunshot was particularly loud.

Roxy flinched, the noise unexpected and assuredly, unwelcome. She raised her hands instinctively and froze in a half crouch. The retort had come from somewhere behind her. As the seconds ticked away at a snail's pace, a thousand different scenarios played out through her mind – and none of them were good. She saw River's pupils dilate as they watched the scene unfold across the charred remains of The Academy. River tightened their grip on Carmine as his eyes bugged and he fought against them with renewed fervor, trying to break free.

Roxy turned around slowly, remaining in a defensive stance, her heart in her throat but ready to fight. *Please, not Suki,* she begged the universe.

Carmine's henchman, JB the Gendarme who had brought shame to the title, lay in a tangled heap on the ground, blood trickling from a wound at his temple. He was clearly unconscious and, quite possibly, dead. And, Suki... well, Suki was holding a gun. It wasn't a very large gun, no, but one that had certainly served its purpose.

It was still smoking.

And it was now pointed directly at Commander Seth Carmine.

"Where the hell did that thing come from?" Carmine squawked, fear causing his voice rise several octaves as he continued to fight against River's hold on him. They hissed in his ear, Carmine flinched and Roxy watched dispassionately as River raked their claws down Carmine's cheek. He began to weep, softly, finally accepting defeat. He wasn't going anywhere.

"I always carry a gun; you piece of shit." Suki shouted, her voice, and her hands, both strong and steady. "Guess it never occurred to you to frisk the 'cripple,' did it?" Her face twisted in anger and the fire in her eyes made her suddenly look very imposing.

Carmine blanched as Suki expertly chambered another round. "But... But JB..."

"But... But JB." Suki mocked. "JB is - my bad, *was* - as dumb as a bag of onions. Was he really the best that you could find for your Gendarme elite?" She laughed. "Not once did he check me for a weapon. He had ample opportunity to frisk me if he wanted to. Old JB here would have flunked out of The Academy within his first semester."

Carmine remained reticent, silenced by fury or fear, perhaps further cowed by Suki's verbal barrage.

It might have been all three. His satisfaction over Sam Sparrow's destruction seemed to have ebbed away.

No, Roxy told herself firmly. *Put Sam out of your mind now, you must focus on Suki.*

"Suki," Roxy cajoled softly, in what she hoped was a reassuring and calming tone. She began a slow approach towards her friend, keeping one eye on the loaded weapon while her mind frantically went over her options might be here. She gave a short shake of her head to River, hoping that the message to stay put got through to them. They needed to keep Carmine subdued. She knew River longed to go to Sam - as much as Roxy did.

"Don't you *Suki* me, Roxy Buckles." Suki's eyes flashed with anger but her gaze did not waver from her target. "Revenge, remember? Finally bringing these lowlifes to justice? Here's our chance. He took so much from us both, Roxy. And Sam." She choked on a sob. "We have to make them pay!"

"You don't want to do this," Roxy prompted.

"Like hell I don't." Suki gave a derisive snort. "Don't you know what he did?"

"I do," Roxy replied softly. "I know everything now."

Suki carried on, not really needing a reply, "Because I know *exactly* what he did. He planted that bomb, he killed all those people, and then he framed Sam for his dirty work. He had one of his goons beat him up – probably this scumbag here - so it looked like he'd been assaulted by Sam before his escaped. It was him all along. Sam was just the scapegoat."

She swallowed with difficulty, trying to control her emotions, and then, her voice dripping with scorn, "The *Commander* didn't mind telling me all the sordid details before you arrived. He was going to kill me anyways, you see."

"I know you want him to pay and he will, I promise you." Roxy insisted as she inched closer. "Just not this way."

"His kind don't understand any other way, Roxy."

"No, Suki, they do not. *But* you are not *his* kind."

Suki wavered for a moment, the gun shook in her hand and the barrel drooped towards the ground. Roxy felt the tight knot of tension in her gut begin to unfurl. She was nearly there; just a few more steps and she'd be close enough to safely disarm Suki. Then it would end.

"You're River Lynx, right?" Suki shouted across the ruins towards the Mauwian sovereign who still held Seth Carmine in a death grip, despite his defeated demeanor. "You have excellent reflexes I would imagine."

River glanced at Roxy, their confusion was evident, but finally they nodded in response to Suki's question. "What you have said is correct, Ms. Kwan."

"Good. You should move. Now."

River did as they were told. Something in Suki's voice telling them that this was not the time to hesitated.

It was not a moment too soon.

Roxy recoiled as the gun blast went off right next to her, an arms length from Suki, loud enough to make her ears ring. She watched in horrified fascination as the bullet slammed into Carmine. He was lifted by the hit, a marionette on a string, before he crumpled to the ground, shrieking as he clutched at the bloody mess that used to be his knee.

Roxy gaped at her friend. "Suki?"

Suki let the gun fall to the ground and then scrubbed her hands along her thighs. She turned towards Roxy as the high-pitched wail of sirens whooped in the distance and the low, steady *chuff, chuff, chuff* of air-ambos hammered the sky as reinforcements drew closer to The Academy, just a little too late to do much good.

With a smirk on her face, Suki tossed her sopping wet hair over her shoulder: "I guess the other bitch got taken care of after all." Her face crumpled. "Roxy. *Sam!*"

Roxy was already halfway across the courtyard, River not far behind her. She knelt on the ground next to Sam and tentatively reached out to touch his face. She snatched her hand back and held it to her mouth, too afraid to speak.

"Roxy?" River stood next to her, their tail flicking with concern. "Is he…?"

"He's so cold, River. So cold."

CHAPTER TWENTY-SIX

Roxy sat, quiet and still, staring into the mirror, not quite recognizing the face staring back at her, though she supposed it must be her. Atop the vanity, sat a small first aid kit. Open, its bandages and plasters spilled out amongst the assorted quick-fix ointments and easy to apply stitch-stickers. She'd refused treatment at the scene, likewise at the hospital, choosing instead to pace the halls with her arms wrapped around herself. Mascara had run in milky gray rivets down her cheeks, a startling contrast against the pale and peaked mask of skin she currently wore.

She couldn't look away.

She raised her eyes to the hair matted with blood, raised a shaky hand to the gash on her forehead. Those hands: crimson stained, dark and crusty around the nail beds where the gore had dried and cracked.

With a small cry, she swept the first aid kit from the desk, its contents flying asunder across the floor. She stood so suddenly that the small chair upon which she had sat fell backwards with a clatter. Wincing, Roxy wrenched the cropped leather jacket from her shoulders and tossed it into a corner. She'd never wear it again. She was no longer wearing her boots. Surely, she must have removed them when she'd arrived at home but she had no recollection of any such event.

She stumbled into the bathroom.

"CoCo, shower mode 5, no auto-shut off this time."

"As you wish Ms. Buckles," came the smooth computerized tones. "Full jets activated. Enjoy."

Stepping into the stall fully clothed, she closed her eyes as the scalding hot water cascaded over her. It pooled for a moment at her feet, pink and foamy, before it circled the drain and disappeared.

The blood and dirt, the sweat and tears – that wasn't all Roxy hoped the water would wash away.

***

"God dammit, Roxy!"

Shivering, Roxy, who lay crumpled on the floor of the marbled shower, still in her clothes, gazed up at Suki, confused. Suki threw a plush white towel around her friends' shoulders and helped her to stand.

"Let's get you out of these wet clothes, hey?" Suki continued in a much gentler tone. "You'll feel much better then. River has ordered us some food."

She led Roxy out of the bathroom and sat her on the bed. "Do you mind if I help you with this?" Asking permission before she tried to peel the sodden clothing from Roxy's quaking body.

"Nothing you haven't seen before, right?" Roxy shot back quickly.

Suki smiled. It was a small spark, but a spark nonetheless. Roxy's reticence had been starting to scare her.

Roxy allowed herself to be undressed though it was difficult for her to feel this vulnerable. Suki dried her briskly with the towel, taking time to squeeze the water gently from her dripping blonde tresses. She helped Roxy slip into a pair of soft pants and a warm, oversized sweater, sliding thick socks onto her feet. Stumbling slightly as she rose from the floor, Suki caught herself on a bedside table. Roxy's hand shot out to steady her.

"Are you sure that you're alright?" Roxy asked, concern evident in her voice, superseding, for the moment, her own discomfort. "It should be *me* looking after *you*, Suki, not the other way around."

Suki stroked Roxy's hand where it lay upon her arm. "Let's look after each other then, shall we?" A smile teased at the corners of her mouth. "Now how about we see what River ordered for us to eat. I'm starving." She frowned. "Fuck. I hope it wasn't fish."

Despite herself, Roxy laughed.

They left the clothes and towels where they lay. A problem for another time, when menial tasks wouldn't feel quite so insurmountable. They closed the door behind them as they headed for the kitchen.

The mouth-watering aromas of *Pad See Eiw*, spicy

Tom yum goong, Khao Pad (a savory fried rice) and Roxy's favorite red curry, *Gaeng Daeng* permeated the condo. Roxy took a deep breath and pressed a hand against her stomach as it grumbled in anticipation of the feast.

"Good. We are ready to eat now." River gestured towards the spread of takeout boxes that covered the entire surface of the countertop island. They held up two paws, both were holding bottles of wine. "And we are also ready to drink."

As River dug into their *Yam Pla Dook Foo* with relish - a dish of Fried Catfish with Green Mango Salad - Suki met Roxy's eyes above the feline's head and quirked an eyebrow. Roxy jammed a spoonful of shrimp soup into her mouth to stifle her laughter.

No, things weren't perfect right now. But they were pretty damned close.

***

River and Suki were discussing the unionization of *SkyShaw* drivers and what it would mean for the future of transportation in the city. They were speaking and gesturing vigorously while shooting Roxy surreptitious glances to ensure that she remained involved in their conversation, keeping her distracted. Roxy was sure Suki and River also had a lot on their mind but she was glad for their company and their concern. She was glad that she wasn't alone. No robo-pet could ever compare.

Suki had been fielding calls and messages all day: reporters, representatives from The PRC; even

Ethel-Beth Lester had called to check on Roxy. The take down of the Commander of The PRC was big news; the corruption that had been exposed was a scandal that reverberated throughout New Cosmos like a shock wave and would continue to do so for ages to come. Those who hadn't heard of Roxy Buckles already, sure knew who she was now.

Finally, Suki had shut down all communication devices and left word at the front desk that no visitors, flowers or packages would be accepted at the condo.

Zillo had called five times, Suki had hesitantly told Roxy as she sloshed more wine into the half empty glass. Roxy nodded in acknowledgment, but turned to look out the window, saying nothing. She made no move to retrieve her wristlet which lay on a side table on the other side of the room, off. In the reflection of the glass, she saw Suki and River exchange a look so she rejoined them in the kitchen. She smiled and smiled and sipped more wine until the whine of a siren, down below, on the streets assaulted her senses. Someone, somewhere else in New Cosmos was also having a bad day too.

Her mind drifted and the sound of River and Suki chatting died away. She could smell the damp earth, saturated from the sudden storm; she could taste the metallic sharpness of iron on her tongue; the pounding of her heart, the rush of blood in her ears.

She could also remember the immense flood of relief she had felt as River had bent over the man who lay prone on the ground only to wave frantically to the first responders, shouting, "He's got a pulse!"

CHAPTER TWENTY-SEVEN

Roxy blinked back to reality.

Suki and River were holding a whispered confer-
ence at the other end of the table, heads bent together,
their backs to Roxy. Just how long had she been lost
in the reverie? She flushed, embarrassed.

"What are you two scheming about now?" Roxy
tried to keep her voice light and airy.

"We were thinking that perhaps it would be a
good idea for you to get away for a bit. Until some of
this fervor dies down." Suki suggested hesitantly.

"What do you mean?" Roxy asked, immediately
suspicious.

"You are everywhere, Roxy. Buckles & Associates
has received 4698 calls in the past twelve hours. When
that CommsLink System went hot, it pinged every
computerized interface on this planet. The driver of
a Transport Barge was close enough that he was able
to broadcast the whole thing as it happened via *Face-
Gram Live*." Suki sighed. "It's gone beyond viral."

"I guess it's good for business?" Roxy joked.

"Roxy, for every one hundred people who love

you, another one hundred hate you. With a passion."
Suki cringed. "We've tried to keep you from the news
reports. The PRC is scrambling right now; the entire
Gendarme has been abolished until they can weed
out the ones who were loyal to Carmine from the
ones who are loyal to the badge. There was a bomb
threat at the Chaffey building just this morning."

"There are some that would have your head on a
silver platter, Roxy." River interjected, blunt as ever.
"It will take time to separate the wheat from the chaff
as Suki has said. You will go underground. Until it is
safe. No contact with anyone. Not even your friend
Zero."

"Zillo." Roxy replied, dryly

River blinked at her. "Yes, that is what I said."

Roxy shook her head. "Okay, okay." She went
silent, processing the information, then squared her
shoulders. "So, what do we do?

"That is where I come in." River replied. "I believe that I can provide a solution to your problem."

Roxy gave a slight nod to show she was listening.

River continued: "You will return with me to
Mauw. No one will know where you have gone ex-
cept the three of us here. We will provide you safe
haven, much as we did with Sam. You will stay as
long as you need to until things calm down here on
Aurora."

Roxy lowered her eyes at the mention of Sam. "I…
I appreciate this very much River but I don't see how
I could possible leave right now. There's too much to

do. Suki can't..."

"With all due respect, Roxy," River interrupted, pupils dilating. "Suki is *more* than capable of handing things here. I believe in her and you should too. She has proven herself time and again."

Suki blushed. Roxy took in the purple and black bruise that had spread across Suki's forehead, the split and swollen lip, the battered knuckles and bandaged wrists, raw from the tape that had bound her to her chair. And yet here she was, still fighting at Roxy's side as always.

"I'm sorry Suki. I don't give you enough credit," Roxy acknowledged, clearing her throat that was suddenly tight with suppressed emotion. "River is right. You *are* more than capable."

"Thank you for saying that, Roxy. Will you go with River? They've arranged transportation for you both. I think this is for the best, at least for now.

"What about you? Will you be safe Suki?"

"Don't worry about me, Roxy. I have everything under control."

"Alright then," Roxy finally agreed, relenting in the face of common sense.

Suki sighed audibly; her relief evident. "Good."

Roxy smirked. "Now, which one of you is going to help me pack?"

***

As Suntwin set, and the last fingers of hazy tangerine caressed the horizon, Roxy and River departed for Mauw. Roxy fell asleep almost instantly; the heavy vibrations of the motor, too much wine and too little sleep, a heady combination.

She stirred just as the ship set down on terra firma; her arrival this time a little less clandestine than the last. River rose sinuously from where they had sat, stretching and yawning broadly. Roxy hadn't been the only one to grab a cat nap on the way to Mauw.

A small group of Mauwian's greeted her and River as they stepped down from the gangplank of the ship. Roxy recognized Bareen, who bowed deeply.

"Welcome back, Ms. Buckles."

"Thank you, Bareen." Roxy wasn't sure if she was supposed to bow back in greeting. Ruffled she did a sort of curtsey which seemed to please both River and Bareen.

River turned to Roxy, "I believe you might also remember Kashmir?"

A younger Mauwian stepped from behind their brethren and hesitantly waved at Roxy. "It is nice to see you Ms. Buckles."

Roxy was quite sure that she would never forget Kashmir.

Smiling, River addressed Roxy once more, "Kashmir was quite eager to prepare lodging for you. They wanted to place you in one of our immediate clusters but I thought perhaps you would prefer some privacy. If you are up to the walk, I can show you to your accommodations."

Tossing her duffel over one shoulder, Roxy summoned a smile. "Lead the way."

***

Roxy climbed a tall ladder and emerged onto an octagonal deck that wrapped around a medium sized treehouse, nestled in the thick branches of the hybrid sequoias that were a signature of Mauw. River had bid her adieu on the ground, having urgent business to attend to; much had accumulated in their absence from heir home planet. The Bastent still required its leader. Perhaps now more than ever.

She poked her head in through the doorway. Kashmir had really outdone themselves. Bowls of fruit and jars of flowers lent a pleasant fragrance to the previously unoccupied abode, giving it an air of hominess. Roxy dropped her bag near the entryway and turned in a full circle. The kitchen was well stocked: bottles of milk and a carafe of thick cream; rice and fish, there was spinach and kale, bunches of fresh herbs and crisp root vegetables; Roxy even thought she spied a bottle of white wine behind several loafs of grainy bread. A small pantry was full of lentils, coffee, flour, sugar and other staples. Roxy would not go hungry.

The small kitchen led way to an equal sized lounge area. A soft throw lay atop an invitingly plush couch; several large cushions and a beanbag chair looked just as comfy. A pile of books sat on a side table next to a potted plant – some type of fern if Roxy was not mistaken – and a small jar of sweets. Through another doorway was the bedroom. A lamp in the corner lit the room softly in rosy hues. Roxy was exhausted; it could have been a dump and it still would have looked like heaven. Roxy had been given directions to a small waterfall nearby where she could clean up. Mauwian's had no need for such amenities but Roxy was certainly thankful to have the option.

Clean now but with little energy for much else, Roxy collapsed into bed, pulling a single sheet over her nakedness. She was asleep within seconds.

*****

A loud thudding sound penetrated the fog of sleep as Roxy struggled to shake off the last vestiges of what had been a very pleasant dream. She stumbled from the bed and headed towards the sound.

"I'm coming, I'm coming!" She muttered as the noise continued.

"Please excuse the very early wakeup call, Roxy but we seem to have a bit of a problem."

"What now?" Roxy groaned and yawned widely, standing in the doorway of the treehouse, the sheet clasped modestly to her chest as the early dawn light bloomed violet and pink behind River Lynx. The look on their face was somber and Roxy quickly came to her senses.

"River," Roxy's voice was now thick with concern as she watched the normally unflappable Mauwian wring her paws. "Tell me what's is going on. Is he...?"

"No, Roxy, not that," they paused. "But, well, it would seem as though Suki Kwan has been arrested."

CHAPTER TWENTY-EIGHT

"A minor inconvenience."

"Suki, they dragged you off in handcuffs." Roxy was incensed. "I'm coming back right now."

Suki, unruffled, laughed at Roxy's indignation. "Stay where you are. It's nothing I can't handle."

"How did this even happen? It's preposterous. It was clearly self-defense."

"Someone got a little too enthusiastic. And now that someone will be riding a desk for the foreseeable future, if they want to keep their job." Suki replied, wryly.

The encrypted software tech that Suki was using to speak with Roxy, that had patched into her usually ineffective at long distances wristlet, emitted a sharp beep indicating that the time for safe and secure conversation would soon pass.

"How did you even get this contraption, Suki? I didn't know such a thing existed. It must be new?" Roxy asked, holding her breath, afraid of the answer but needing to know all the same.

Suki hesitated. "Zillo," she whispered. "I'm sorry

Roxy. I felt really terrible so I returned one of his calls. All I told him was that you were okay and that you were safe. I didn't say a word about where you were or even that you'd gone off planet, but he's smart and I think he read between the lines. He wanted to help. He's a good guy."

"I know." Roxy demurred.

Beep.

"I think our time is coming to an end," Suki interjected. "Look everything is under control, I'm fine and I can promise you no one else will try and lock me up again. I can get back to fixing things up around here. And then we can get you back. I don't want you to worry about it anymore, got it?"

"Got it. But… you're sure that you're okay, Suki?"

There was a long pause, then Suki giggled. "If I'm being honest Roxy, and please, I hope you don't think badly of me when I say this but… I am fairly certain this has been the most exciting week of my entire life."

Roxy gave a throaty chuckle. She could definitely understand that.

Beep.

Sobering quickly, and before she could lose her nerve, she asked, "Have you been able to see him?"

"No, but not for a lack of trying. They wouldn't allow it. Something about following protocols… they wouldn't give me a lot of details."

"He's… he's going to make it though, right?"

The device gave one final ear-splitting beep and

then the line went dead.

***

Roxy spent her time on Mauw trying to do the one thing that she was not very good at: relaxing. The time went by slowly; the first week that she was there felt indeterminable, she felt sluggish like she was trying to push her way through syrup. But it was not entirely unpleasant once she got into a routine and stopped feeling so sorry for herself. She went for long walks, exploring, and collected wild flowers that she delivered to the Mauwian elders. She cooked elaborate meals for herself, read books for pleasure and somehow managed to keep that one fern alive. She went swimming at the falls nearly every day, floating on her back in the heady rays of Suntwin, her eyes closed, striving to keep her mind blank. To just enjoy.

The bottle of wine remained at the back of the fridge.

She regularly attended meetings of The Bastent, though she mostly sat at the back of the room, listening quietly and taking it all in. Roxy would never be the type of person who would completely turn the other cheek in a dangerous situation but she was beginning to realize that, perhaps, there were a few other things she could try first rather than storming in, half cocked, guns ablaze. It was quite the epiphany for her.

She had long chats with River; there was an easy trust between the two now and Roxy was learning that friendship meant an equal give and take and that she didn't always have to be in control. And that sometimes people were more than capable of taking care of themselves.

The seasons changed but it was subtle shift on the planet Mauw. The days got a little bit shorter and a little bit darker, a cooler wind blew every now and again but everything else remained much the same. On Mondays, Kashmir came by Roxy's treehouse. They were attempting to teach Roxy an elaborate board game that was comparable to chess and, while the skills were slow in coming to Roxy, she kept trying; Kashmir was a patient teacher.

It was during one of these sessions that Kashmir, finally having worked up the courage, asked, "Ms. Roxy, will you teach me how to fight. I want to be able to defend my brethren. No matter what it takes."

Roxy contemplated her answer, knowing that the eager young Mauwian was at an impressionable age. "Well, Kashmir, fighting isn't always the answer." Roxy surprised even herself with that response. "There are many other ways to defend yourself, and your friends, without killing. Justice… it isn't always so black and white."

And, so, that was how Roxy ended up teaching mixed martial arts to the oldest of the kittens, twice a week, in the community hall. They were rowdy but Roxy appreciated their enthusiasm and it gave her something physical to do. She felt alive.

It was, all at once, the strangest, but also the most normal time, of Roxy's entire life.

***

Roxy had dragged the beanbag chair and a soft blanket to the balcony. She sat watching the day reluctantly give way to night, the blanket across her lap as she nursed a cup of lukewarm herbal tea. She heard the soft sound of company padding its way up the ladder. River emerged through entryway; a shawl wrapped around their shoulders.

"River, to what do I owe the pleasure? Not that I'm complaining now, mind you." She felt her smile falter as River stood there, stoic faced.

"It's over Roxy."

Roxy rose from her beanbag, the blanket falling to the deck to pool around her feet. She had longed to hear those words. She was afraid to speak, lest she break the spell and wake up. She had now been living on Mauw for six months… while things had gone straight to hell and back on Aurora.

"Really?" she whispered, breathless, hand at her throat.

River nodded. "Suki has sent word. It's safe now, Roxy. You can finally go home."

EPILOGUE

"Load 'em up!"

The call echoed down the long bare hallway and out into the obscurity of night as a line of chained and shackled prisoners were led one by one from a squat brick building and across a darkened and rutted tarmac. Awaiting them with open doors, lights ablaze and motors humming, was *The Quentin*, a passenger carrier specifically equipped to safely and effectively transport convicts.

A man at the end of the line limped along slowly in his ankle restraints; his drab, faded grey prison uniform and black canvas sneakers were not at all like the clothes he had grown accustomed to as a part of his lavish lifestyle. There were no extravagantly tailored suits or costly *crocator* shoes where he was going. No meals paid for on the taxpayer's dime, no hush money deposited into various off-planet accounts. It would be a whole new ballgame.

"Move it along there, *Commander*," Fredriks sneered with as much malice as he could muster. Being one of the newly appointed Gendarme under the direction of Hadrian Durand, Freddie Fredriks had little time for scum like the former leader of The PRC. He prodded Seth Carmine sharply from behind with a long black baton, a quick jab to the ribs. "We ain't got all day."

"My knee." Carmine whined, his face screwed up piteously, lower lip trembling as he sought sympathy from the guard.

"Barking up the wrong tree, mate." The guard remarked scornfully, looking down his nose at Carmine, of disgust written all over his face. "You're lucky that little lady didn't shoot you a wee bit higher. Then you'd really have something to complain about." He smirked. "Now get a move on before I *make* you move."

Each prisoner was led aboard the ship and taken to their individually assigned cryo-pods. Once inside, they would remain in stasis for the entirety of their journey. And quite a long journey it would be.

Brig-5, the prison planet, was located in the X-Sector – an otherwise undeveloped region at the furthest reaches of the solar system. It would take the better part of a year before they would reach their destination, and equally as long to return to Aurora.

A short while later, all twelve prisoners had been prepped for the trip, locked within their cryo-pods and sent off to dreamland, despite their loud and lengthy protestations of innocence. Fuel reserves had been filled and final checks had been done on *The Quentin* as per the pilots' instructions. It would ensure a smooth and problem free foray into the beyond.

Take off was now imminent.

"Captain? We're ready when you are." Fredriks called out, speaking for the rest of the small crew that would accompany the ship on its excursion. There were not many that would volunteer to take this particular job but for those willing to give up two entire years of their lives, the pay would be quite handsome indeed.

"Thank you, Fredriks." Sam Sparrow stepped out from the cockpit, handsome in his trim pilots' uniform, a line of gleaming gold and silver medals pinned across his breast pocket. "Certainly glad to have you along for the trip. I know it must be very difficult to leave your family behind."

"Aye, they'll keep. I'm glad to be here, Captain. And yourself, do you got anyone waitin' for you when you return?"

Sam gazed thoughtfully at Fredricks for a moment and then gave a small, clipped smile as he turned to re-enter the cockpit: "I sure hope so Fredriks. I sure hope so."

MORE SCI-FI FROM ENGEN

Fans of the From the Rock series should be sure to check out *Slipstreamers*, a new monthly adventure series from Engen Books. The series follows the adventures of Cassidy Cane as she slips through dimensions to strange new worlds, all in hopes of finding cures for the problems that plague her home Earth.

Each episode will be written by a new talent from the Atlantic Canadian genre fiction scene, giving a fresh take to each new world that Cassidy visits.

Featuring the words of many different From the Rock contributors and the astonishing art of Ariel Marsh, this series is not to be missed!

ABOUT THE AUTHOR

Nicole Little lives in St. John's. Her short stories have appeared in twelve anthologies thus far including five collections with Engen Books and seven collections from Australian publisher Black Hare Press.

Her fiction has won several competitions including the June 2018 Kit Sora prize for her flash fiction piece "Sweet Sixteen;" her short story "Doxxed" placed 3rd in the Writers Alliance of Newfoundland and Labrador's "A Nightmare on Water Street: Scary Story Reading" in October 2018 and her three-sentence horror story, "Tasty Babies" earned her the much-coveted Hell Hare award from Black Hare Press in January 2020.

Her first novella, *The Lotus Fountain: A Slipstreamers Adventure*, was shortlisted for the Write Project Book of the Year 2020 Award.

In her spare time, Nicole has either a pen in her hand or her nose in a book. She is married with two daughters.